Shemeka Mitchell's

Loving

LESLIE

Printed in the U.S.A.
First Printing, 2016
Shemeka Mitchell
ISBN-13: 978-0692676141 (Custom)
ISBN-10: 0692676147
Dreyne Publications
2920 W Lynn ST
Springfield, MO 65802
http://mshemeka.wix.com/meka
https://www.facebook.com/AuthorSMitchell/
https://twitter.com/shemitchell

About The Author

Shemeka grew up in a small town in Arkansas and has always had a passion for reading and writing. After being diagnosed with Lupus, and unable to work, she decided that it was time to work on her novels. She wrote her very first novel in 2013 and after being encouraged by a dear friend, she pursued her dreams by learning to necessary tools to start her writing journey. Proud to be a published author, Shemeka is also an advocate for Lupus Awareness. Currently, Shemeka resides in southwest Missouri with her two children: D'Andre and Blossom.

Books by Shemeka Mitchell
Love, Lies, and Loyatly Series
Everlasting Love -1
Tainted Lies - 2
Blind Trust - 3
Endless Love - 4
Misplaced Loyalty – 5
Rendezvous In Vegas
Vindictive

Chapter 1

August 2009

Leslie Adams caught herself dozing off while listening to an irate customer complaining about how high her phone bill was at the moment. She wanted, badly, to tell the lady that if she paid her bill on time she wouldn't have all of those late fees added on each and every month. She knew that it was against company policy to be rude to a customer even though they deserved it at times. So she held her composure and explained it to the customer in the nicest way possible.

The woman asked to speak with a manager and Leslie quickly passed her on to the next department. On days like this, she despised her job at the phone company. It was sunny Friday afternoon, mid August and it was a scorcher. She couldn't wait to get off work and begin her fun weekend of relaxation. A few of her friends were having a long overdue get together tonight and she had been looking forward to it for a couple of weeks. They hadn't really hung out together since the barbecue she hosted on the 4th of July. It was long overdue in her book. She lived for the groups "kickin it" sessions.

As soon as the clock struck four, she logged out of the program, hopped up from her seat and headed for the door, not waiting to chat with anyone. It wasn't that she didn't like her coworkers; she just didn't have any conversation for them on this particular day. She was more than ready to chill with her real friends. Not to say that the friends from work weren't original friends, well wait, that was exactly how she felt about her coworkers.

They wanted to discuss one another's business in details and she preferred having no part in the workplace gossip mill. Once she got to her car her reflection in the window depressed her something serious. A groan escaped her mouth as she took in the sight. Her hair was a frizzy mess and her make-up was barely there. She ran her fingers through her long, thick, curly brown mane trying to tame it which was useless as always. Leslie had spent an entire hour on her head that morning with hopes of not having to do it after work. It was just her luck that the air conditioner at work had chosen this day to play out.

All that time spent flat ironing her hair had officially gone down the drain with the heat. She jumped into her old 1994 Geo Tracker and headed home to try and repair the damage before meeting up with her friends. She still had to go to the restaurant to pick up her order and then to the liquor store to get some drinks. They all had decided to bring a dish and drinks, sit back, play some games, drink a lot, eat a little, watch some movies, and just enjoy one another's company. Leslie raced up to her apartment and flung the door open, not bothering to lock it when it closed. She went straight to the bathroom and turned on the shower. She adored her bathroom. It was done in different shades of blue with pictures of sea creatures on the walls and the shower curtain. Dolphins were the majority. They were on the soap dispenser and the tooth brush holder. Even the light blue fluffy towels had a dolphin on each one. After a quick shower, she got started on her hair, attempting to have some sort of control over the fussy mess. It took her thirty minutes to realize that she was fighting a lost cause. An up do was all that she really had time for. In the bedroom, she grabbed a light brown maxi dress and a pair of brown sandal heels.

Her make-up was minimal. Leslie was afraid the heat would work against her even more if she went overboard. Clinique's Happy was her favorite fragrance and she applied a generous amount to her body. She had been in love with that perfume ever since she discovered it at the age of twenty one and she was still rocking it ten years later. She took in her 5'6 frame. Leslie did a slow spin to see how the back looked. She ran her hand across her hips and smiled. Her New Year's resolution was paying off big time. She was in the best shape of her life and her skin had a very healthy glow. She discovered that working out was a great stress reliever for her and she enjoyed it a lot more than she ever thought she would. After looking in the mirror and determining that her look was complete, she headed out the door, ready to begin her weekend!

Chapter 2

Keith Lawson walked around the house inspecting each and every corner of the place. He approved, everything was at least decent. A three-bedroom house with all males could become a little messy at times. He wanted to make sure there at least weren't any droplets of urine on or around the toilet. He also made sure that each bathroom was properly stocked with tissue, hand soap, and clean towels. His roommates were doing their own thing in preparation of their guests. They had a fun night planned with the girls and he couldn't wait. It had been a long week at the office where he worked. He'd just been promoted to human resource manager and he enjoyed his job, but since they were in the process of hiring new employees, he had his work cut out for him. It beat the hell out of going to some loud, crowded nightclub Sam always wanted to drag them to.

Keith had known Telvin Jameson, a tall light skin dude that had the build of a football player, for most of his life. They had been best friends ever since the second grade, every since his parents moved in next door to the Lawsons'.

Keith and Telvin bonded immediately over that first summer, spending all of their time outside playing ball or riding bikes. When the school year started, they were closer that ever and continued to claim each other as brothers. They met Sam Williams during their college years at MSU. Sam was the odd ball of the group. He was short and chubby, but that didn't take away from his appeal. Women always fell for him, saying that he was adorable like a cuddly teddy bear. It didn't hurt that he had hazel eyes and wavy hair. His skin ebony skin was flawless.

It was a chance meeting between Sam and Keith. They were both dating the same girl without knowing about it. When they found out about one another, they got together and formed a plan to get even with the girl, who brought them closer after they spent the night laughing at the young woman's expense. From then on it was the three of them. The trio formed an alliance and had been together ever since. They hadn't always lived together. Sam had a very serious relationship with a woman named Lisa, whom Keith could not stand. Keith felt that she was shallow and very superficial. He kept his mouth shut about his best friend's love until he noticed how she was spending his money on other men.

Even though it broke Sam's heart, they performed an intervention and made him see reasoning. When Sam worked up the courage to confront her, she laughed in his face and told him that he was stupid for not realizing it sooner. It was then that they decided to get a place together. With Telvin losing his job and not being able to keep his apartment, he readily jumped on the opportunity to save some money. It all worked out great. They enjoyed hanging out and reliving their college days with the exception of being grown men holding down full time jobs. They each had known the ladies that were coming over for a while also.

All of them often got together to hang out when given the chance. Keith had known Leslie the least amount of time. She was friends with his cousin, Darcy Lawson, which was one of the ladies coming over, along with Bre Davis and her friend, Ashlyn Kennedy. Keith shook his head at the thought of Ashlyn. She wasn't shy by a long shot. She was always throwing herself at him every available opportunity. Her body was banging and she had a cute face with medium length black silky hair that grazed her shoulders from time to time. He knew that her mother was from the Philippines and her dad was a black man. If he was honest, she was down right gorgeous, but her attitude took away from her beauty tremendously. In her mind, she was the best looking woman in Missouri.

It seemed as if it was her mission to claim Keith as her own and he was having no parts of it. He preferred being single instead of the trials of dealing with an unstable woman. Keith did another walk through and decided that things were as clean as they were going to get.

"Yo Keith, are you planning on hooking up with Ashlyn tonight?" Telvin asked him as soon as he entered the living room.

Keith smirked at him, "What do you think?"

"Man I don't know. She is fine as hell. I don't see why you wouldn't have fun with her." The laughter was evident in his eyes and Keith noticed it before Telvin could turn away.

"Why don't you hook up with her?" He threw out at his friend.

"Oh no, I don't do relationships anymore. One heart break is enough for this year. Maybe I will jump back in the ring next year," he said while clutching his chest. Keith threw a pillow at him and he caught it.

"How are you going to put her off on me? You know she isn't my type." Keith was not at all interested in anything Ashlyn had to offer. She did nothing for him, little did she know. He thought about it for a moment, maybe he should inform her of it and maybe then she would leave him the hell alone and stop being a fucking nuisance to everyone.

"Man, do you even have a type?" Sam said as he rolled his eyes at Keith. Keith knew instantly that he was recalling their college years when they all were a little one the wild side of things.

"Yeah, I do and when I find her, I'll let you know." He said as he heard the doorbell alerting them that their guests had begun to arrive. Sam walked from the kitchen and answered the door. Ashlyn breezed in with an air of confidence and Keith shuddered inwardly. He wondered why Bre insisted on bringing her to hang out with them when not one of them really warmed up to her. She usually did or said something to piss someone off each and every time she imposed on their outings. Ashlyn made her way over to Keith, passing by Sam and Telvin on her way to him.

"Keith, it's so delightful to see you," she squealed excitedly. She grabbed him in an embrace and Keith spied his boys stifling the laughter that was on their faces.

"It's nice to see you," he replied while shooting daggers at his friends.

8

"Why haven't you called me?" She asked him as soon as he released her. It wasn't a secret that she had a thang for Keith. She was infatuated with his looks. He was a sexy chocolate brother with dark piercing eyes. She told anyone that would listen about how one day she was going to be wrapped up in those big strong arms of his. Keith knew her interests were only superficial. She was known for being a gold digger and he was sure that was all she wanted from him. Well, that and the ten inches he packed in his pants. When it came to women, they tended to run their mouth just a little too much. She'd heard about his sex game and now she wanted to experience it for herself. He just couldn't bring himself to sleep with her. She was not the kind of woman a man wanted to have a relationship with, quite the opposite.

"I've been real busy with work and all," he informed her as he walked to the door to see what was keeping Bre. "Where's Bre?"

"Oh she is getting the things from the trunk," she said as she flopped down on the sofa. Keith frown at her and shook his head. He made his way outside to see if Bre needed any help. She was bent over the trunk attempting to situate everything so that one trip was all it took.

"Hey girl, how are you?" Keith called out to her as he began gathering up the bags she had brought.

"Hey Keith, how are you doing? I see Ashlyn had the decency to let y'all know to come and help me."

"Nope, she sure didn't. I came out here because I figured you did need some help. She sat her ass on the sofa and started flipping through the channels. Why do you always bring her with you? I mean I know that's your girl and all, but she is a little nerve wrecking," he slowed his step so that they could have a few minutes to chat before entering the house.

"I know she can be a bit much, but sometimes I feel sorry for her. She always manages to catch me when I'm planning a night out. She's like a stalker and I think I'm her only friend." Bre admitted to Keith.

"That's why she does it. Just so you can feel sorry and then you will allow her to follow you on your outings. This is supposed to be a friendly atmosphere with just us. You know, real friends, not impostors."

"I know, I know. I'm sorry, I couldn't say no." Keith put him arms on her shoulders and gave her a squeeze. Bre had been hanging with them since their college years. They all thought she was a dime, but they valued her friendship more than trying to fuck. Bre was a tall chick standing at almost 6 feet. Her skin was the color of a shiny penny with eyes the same. She wore her hair in a short choppy style. She was an all around lovey to all that cross her path. Keith assumed that was the reason for Ashlyn latching on to her the way she did. They all knew that Ashlyn was a shitty ass friend to her but she'd stick up for the chick each and every time one of them said anything negative about her home girl. That's why Keith had to hold his tongue before he said too much.

"Hey, it's cool. Sorry for attacking you. I have no right to judge your friend." He told her as he made a mental note to chill on talking about her girlfriend and be on his best behavior for the rest of the night.

"It's all good. I know you do it because you care and I am beginning to see what you mean. As a matter of fact, I told her on the way over here that if she starts acting up, I'm going to put her ass in a cab and send her home. We are going to have a superb time and no drama is wanted nor needed." She said with her head held high as she made her way into the house.

"Thanks for helping me with the bags, Ashlyn," Bre called out to her.

"Oh girl I'm sorry. I forgot," she pleaded with her friend.

"Yeah, sure you did," Sam whispered over to Telvin who chuckled slightly.

"So, who else is going to be here tonight?" Ashlyn asked as if she had the right to know all of the details.

"Leslie and Darcy should be here any minute now," Keith answered her without noticing the sour expression on her face. He was on his way to put the drinks in the fridge and the food on the table.

"What did you bring to tonight's festivities Ash," Sam asked her. He really didn't like the woman either. She was nice to look at, but only from a distance at best. The way she threw herself at men was not attractive at all to them.

"I didn't know I was supposed to bring something. What, don't you think my presence is enough?" She batted her eyes at him. Sam blushed and turned to walk away from her. Just then they heard the arrival of the others.

"Hey baby cousin," Keith said as he grabbed Darcy in a big bear hug, "how's it going, baby girl?" Keith and Darcy grew up together and they were the closest out of all the cousins in their family. She was a beautiful chocolate woman with short black hair. He never knew her to let it grow out because she'd always say that she hated hair. She was on the short side with a huge attitude to balance it all out. He'd been attempting to hook her up with Telvin for the longest, but they went together like oil and water. One was bound to piss the other one off in minutes. If in a relationship, Keith could imagine them going at it on a daily basis, so he chilled on trying to be a match maker. He loved his cousin and he wanted what was best for both of them even if it meant them not exploring a relationship with one another.

"You are only a couple of years older than me," she protested as she hugged him back. He released her and turned his attention to Leslie.

"Hey Miss Leslie, how are you?" He asked her with a smile on his face. His eyes roamed over her body briefly taking in her nice plush curves. She looked simply delectable and that short dress gave him plenty to view. Her wild curls where piled up in a ponytail and her skin looked so soft that he wanted to reach out and touch just to verify it. As she walked past him, he caught her scent, she always smelled so good to him. He wanted to bury his nose in her neck and inhale deeply.

"I'm good, how are things going tonight? She said as she looked around him and caught sight of Ashlyn. A frown adorned her beautiful face immediately. Keith laughed and said, "I see you spotted our uninvited guest." Leslie was not fond of Ashlyn in the least bit and Keith was well aware of that fact.

"Ugh, if I'd known she was going to be here, I would have stayed home." She told him. Her beautiful face held a grimace as if she was in pain at the sight of the other woman. Keith held in his laughter and shook his head.

"Yeah and I would have came and got your ass. If we have to suffer, so do you," he said as he led them to the

12

kitchen. He looked in the bag that Leslie handed him. Once he examined what was inside, he held it to his chest and closed his eyes, "Um-mm, a woman after my own heart!" He exclaimed.

"Whatever Keith, it is not only for you. You do have to share it," Leslie scolded him.

"But I don't want to share. Well maybe with you since you bought it." He wagered.

Darcy snatched the bag away from him careful not to ruin the cake, "Oh no cousin, you can not have all of this goodness to yourself. You have definitely got to share. You know what they say, Nothing is better than sex except chocolate and I know I'm in a drought. So I'm going to need at least three slices."

"And the same goes for me," Leslie joined in.

"What are y'all talking about?" Ashlyn asked as she entered the kitchen. She spotted the chocolate cake and headed straight to Darcy. "Oh, I love chocolate cake. Can I have a piece?" Even though she made a show of asking, she didn't wait for permission before taking the cake out of Darcy's hands and heading to the counter to cut a slice.

Keith reached out and swiped the cake before she could open the container, "I'm sorry, but this belongs to me and I don't do sharing," he told her.

"Not even with me? I thought we were better than that." She pouted at him and he pointedly ignored her and her look. She was already on that bullshit and he wasn't having any part of it, especially not with Leslie eyeing the interaction with so much intent. He caught Leslie's eye before responding to Ashlyn. She gave him a wink before turning her attention to the woman of the minute.

13

"Leslie brought it for me because she knows it's my favorite. No one is getting a piece unless I give the okay," he let her know that she wasn't as slick as she thought. Her implications meant nothing to him. A relationship between them was not possible in his mind. He often detested her and her attitude.

"Well, okay, I see how you are. Just for that I may not let you have any of this tonight and I had planned on giving you all of it." She stated then turned on her heels and headed back to the living room while Keith shook his head at her retreating form. Like he really wanted some anyways, he thought to himself with a chuckle.

"Dang Keith, you better go and kiss up to your girl," Leslie said to him. She knew for a fact that he couldn't stand the thought of being with the woman, but that didn't stop her from instigating.

"You know she isn't my girl," he rolled his eyes at her and clicked his tongue like she always did to him. "I don't do superficial, but if you play nice, I might do you." Leslie's eyes almost bulged out of her head at that. She was stunned into silence by his words. Little did Keith know she'd often had fantasies of running her tongue along the tribal tattoo that ran from his biceps to the beginning of his chest. She'd even imagined tracing the panther within. She recalled going with him to get it done.

That was the very first time she saw him without his shirt and she almost fainted on the spot. Keith's body was to die for. All hard and muscular is the best description she had of his body. He took pride in it and anyone could tell. What really made her feelings for him develop is when he told her the meanings of the ink he chose and how it signified strength, power, and loyalty.

"I think you guys would make a lovely couple," Darcy said to Keith and Leslie giggled. He looked from Darcy to Leslie and cocked his head to the side.

"Oh you two got jokes? Okay, just remember that pay back is a mutha," he warned them as he placed the cake on the counter and pulled them both into the living room.

"Alright y'all, let's get this thing popping," Bre yelled over the music Sam had turned on.

For the next hour the friends ate, drank, and danced on and off until they were all sweating. Telvin turned the music down a little and they started up a card game then moved on to dominoes. Everyone was having a great time. Ashlyn was behaving for the first time and no one had words with her. As the night wore on and the buzzes' were in full effect, they decided to play Truth or Dare. Some told truths, some chose dares. Ashlyn was the next person to go and Keith was her object.

"Truth or dare?" She asked him with a sly smile on her face.

"Truth," he answered, not really wanting any parts of her dares.

"Are you afraid of my dares?" she asked him.

"Nope, I'm not, ask your question," he insisted.

"How many times have you made a woman orgasm in one night?" she licked her lips as she waited for him to answer. Everyone else burst out laughing at the question.

"Damn, she on it," Sam yelled.

"I want to know what I'm going to be working with," she replied full of confidence that she would be spending the night wrapped up in his arms, in his bed.

"Man, answer the question," Telvin barked.

"Um, maybe five times," Keith was deep in thought trying to remember the exact number.

Leslie had a look of surprise on her face, "You know you lying. You chose truth. You are supposed to tell the damn truth." Her buzz was in full force just like everyone else. Otherwise she wouldn't have been as bold as to call him out like that. That outburst made the others laugh even more.

Keith looked over at Leslie, "Why do you think I'm lying?"

"I mean really, how often do men take the time to actually make the woman cum? Most of you guys just want to get your nut so you can go to sleep. Some of you don't even know how to work it while others want to punish it, make it so you can't walk the next day. Hell, women want to feel good. Why we got to be punished?" Leslie reasoned with Keith while Bre agreed with her.

"Girl, I know what you mean. Sometimes it just ain't worth getting dirty over." She slurred slightly.

"You need to give up your keys. You aren't going anywhere tonight," Telvin said to her. She huffed and puffed but she gave him her keys without uttering another word. She knew the rules. Even though fun was on their minds, they didn't approve of letting friends get behind the wheel while intoxicated.

"Anyways, Leslie, why don't you believe that it is possible for a man to give a woman multiple orgasms?" Keith was intrigued as to why she thought that way. He always made certain that his partner experienced the utmost pleasure while with him. Giving women his all gave him a major thrill.

"I didn't say all of that. I know it is possible, but most men don't take the time out to explore a woman's body. That's all I'm saying." She replied shyly.

"Okay, my turn. Leslie, truth or dare," Keith challenged her. He spotted the fear in her eyes and knew she wouldn't be choosing dare anytime soon.

"Truth," she was terrified of his dare. His look told her that he was up to something. What, she just didn't know. So she figured she'd be better off playing it safe instead of putting herself out there. Well, at least until a few drinks later.

"How many orgasms have you had in one night?" He asked her, suddenly interested in the answer.

"Um, maybe one," she felt the heat in her cheeks. Ashlyn laughed out loud as if that was the funniest thing she'd ever heard. All eyes turned to her, waiting for the laughter to subside.

"You must have been messing with some lame ass men then. I need to cum at least twice before the guy even thinks about nuttin. Keith, are you taking notes?" She winked at him. He didn't see it because he had returned his attention to Leslie.

"So you are sexually deprived?" His eyes held hers, daring her to confirm his suspicion. He knew it wasn't wise of him to put her on the spot like that. She might shy away from the challenge and their friendship if he wasn't careful of his approach.

"I wouldn't say all of that," she stammered, picking up her glass of wine and taking a huge gulp.

"I would," He knew she was nervous, but he also observed something else flickering in her eyes, interest maybe.

"Anyways my turn," Darcy piped in breaking the eye contact between Keith and Leslie.

"Oh lardy, here we go," Ashlyn started. She rolled her eyes and took a deep breath.

"Trick, shut up and let her ask the question," Bre said to her surprise. Ashlyn was stunned into silence by her friend speaking to her in that manner. Keith wanted to bust a serious gut at the exchange between the two of them.

"Keith, truth or dare," asked Darcy.

"Damn, what's up with y'all picking on me tonight?" he asked them all with a shake of his head.

"Shut up and pick," she told him as she hit him playfully on the leg.

"Okay okay, truth," he gave in to her demands. Darcy had some shit up her sleeve and he was game for it. If he played his cards right, she just might help him concur the infamous Leslie on this night, he thought to himself.

"Have you ever thought about making Leslie cum?" Darcy asked as she tried hard to contain her laughter. She knew the answer. She figured it was time Leslie knew it.

"Darcy," Leslie shouted at her friend who had let the laugh escape. Leslie's beautiful face was on fire. Keith thought the sight was adorable. He knew she was sweet and innocent. Her blushing validated his point even more so.

"Yes, I have." Keith answered without skipping a beat. Leslie forced herself not to look in his direction as the game

18

went on with some crazy dares. His eyes never left her for a moment. He was patiently awaiting his turn. It fell back on Keith and he picked Leslie as his victim.

"Truth or dare, Leslie," he asked her. She finally looked at him and saw a flicker of something in his eyes. Her heart skipped a beat and she felt bold.

"Dare," she eyed him as she answered.

"I bet I can make you cum no less than four times. I dare you to let me prove it to you," his look challenged her. The room grew quiet while they waited for her to respond.

"And what if you don't?" She asked him with her voice trembling.

"If I don't, then I will pay you $1,000.00." he knew it was time to step his game up. His reputation was now on the line. It wasn't as if he thought she'd go around telling her business, he just wanted it to be good for her, the best she ever had.

"Damn, you got to be shitting me! I've been practically throwing myself at you all night." Ashlyn whined. No one paid any attention to her as they watched the interaction between Keith and Leslie.

"But I promise you that it will happen," his need to please her was intense. He wanted her in his bedroom instantly. He licked his lips as he thought about tasting her and his desire increased ten folds. "What do you say? Do you accept my dare?" He tilted his head to the side and waited for her to answer.

"Oh shit, I want to see how this plays out," Darcy bounced in her seat as if she was watching a movie.

"Keith man, I think you scared her," Sam called out drawing a chuckle from Telvin.

"I'm not scared!"

"Well answer me then," Keith taunted her with his eyes.

"I accept," she gave in to him and the desire that was burning in the pits of her core. He stood, walked over to her, took her hand and led her to his room without saying a word to their friends. Once in the room, he pushed her down on the bed.

"Are you sure you want to do this?" he asked, sitting down on the bed beside her.

"It is a little too late to back out now."

"It's never too late. I don't want you to do anything that you aren't comfortable with. I need for you to be sure." He let his hand caress her inner thigh as his lips brushed against her neck.

"I...I'm sure," she finally told him. He turned her face to him and slowly brought his lips to hers. Upon contact her blood pressure shot through the roof. His kisses were sweet with a slight taste of wine and chocolate. He let his kisses drop to her neck.

"You smell delightful," he whispered against her neck.

"Thank you," her mind was in a puddle. She didn't want to talk. All she wanted to do was feel and experience what he was offering to her. She felt his hand come up to cup her full breast through the thin fabric of her dress while his other hand caressed her back. He eased one of her straps down to reveal a plump breast. He then leaned down to capture the dark brown pebble between his moist lips.

As soon as he made contact, she released the moan that she was holding in. She raised her hand to his head to keep him in place for fear of him stopping the sweet pleasure he was inflicting upon her body. He continued on for a while then he pulled down the other strap. She was exposed from the waist up. He let his hands touch her body as his eyes took in her demeanor. He knew she wanted more, but he was going to take his time.

"Slide up on the bed," he instructed. She did as she was told. He removed her dress the rest of the way and threw it to the side. His hands grasped her ankles and trailed their way up to her thong. He slid his fingers in the waistband and took them off with ease. Once she was completely nude, he stood at the foot of the bed to shed his own clothes. He made his way back to her, kissing his way up to her lips. Their tongues touched for the first time. The kiss grew more demanding and she could feel him right in her apex. Her body was hungry for him and she tried to adjust herself to him so that she could take him in. He caught her hips and stilled her.

"My show baby," He told her and she let her head fall back against the pillow as his fingers entered her warm spot. His touch was soft and slow, but the more she moved, the harder his touch became. He kept up the pace until she felt a familiar sensation building in her center. She tried to contain her moans because of their predicament as her first orgasm found its way out.

"One," was all he said before kissing her silly. His tongue flickered over her body until he came to the object of his desire. He breathed in her scent as his placed kisses around her center. When she felt she couldn't withstand it any longer, his tongue invaded her walls making her scream out with pleasure.

"Ohhhhh," she cried while gripping his head. He lapped up all of her earlier juices while creating more. The only thing in her mind was the things he was doing to her. With each stroke of his tongue, she felt herself on the verge of another orgasm and she was shocked at the way her body was responding to him. He focused solely on her bud and the dam broke. Her legs trembled and he gripped them both to keep her in place.

"Two," he said as his warm breath washed over her opening. Her taste was unlike anything he'd ever had the pleasure of tasting before. Her smell was like an aphrodisiac to his mind. He was high on lust.

"Keith," she gasped. Her heart was beating rather rapidly. She thought that she was on the verge of passing out.

"We still have at least two more to go, Leslie." He had no intentions of letting her out of this room without proving to her that all men weren't selfish when it came to sex. Besides, he was thoroughly enjoying himself. She tasted delectable and he wanted more of her. He pushed her knees up to her chest as he let his tongue wander over her. Once he had her to the brink of another climax, he raised up, leaned over to his nightstand to grab a condom from the drawer.

"Let me," she pleaded as she took it from him. Ripping it open, she rolled it up his shaft while he watched on. He'd had women perform that same act before, but when Leslie did it, it did something to him. It made him even harder if that was at all possible. He eased himself into her opening going slow to allow her body time to adjust to the width of him. She was tight and oh so wet. His eyes rolled back in his head with each push. When he was completely in, he felt her

22

muscles constricting around him and it stole his breath momentarily.

"Leslie," he moaned. She pulled his mouth to hers as her tongue invaded it. He allowed her to taste her essence from his tongue. Her nails scraped across his back making him drive deeper inside of her. He was amazed at the way Leslie felt wrapped around his shaft. She was soaking wet and very tight. He had to calm his nerves if he expected to last. He closed his eyes and counted to thirty before moving at all.

"Keith," she cried out as he buried himself inside of her wetness. He groaned before continuing. At this rate, he'd be damn if he lasted longer than ten minutes. He'd never felt anything quite as good as the way she fit all snug around him. He was losing control as he worked his way in and out of her body. She locked her arms around him as he took her to paradise over and over again.

Chapter 3

Lying on her side with Keith spooning her from behind, Leslie's mind replayed the night over and over. Disbelief rolled through her body, as the images of the different positions he had her in, broke through. The delightful soreness in her body proved to be a new experience for her and she found herself enjoying the delicious feeling of being thoroughly sexed. She felt her face flaming as she remembers the way he'd basically told everyone in the room they would be having sex. She figured that it was going to take a while for her to be able to live it down because her girlfriends were sure going to want to hear details as soon as possible. Plus, she wasn't sure she was up to facing Keith after the way he had her behaving. Thinking that a quick escape was the best plan of action, Leslie attempted to ease out of Keith's embrace without rousing him. To her dismay, his arm tightened around her waist.

"Where are you going?" he mumbled sleepily.

"I'm going to head home," she told him trying to work her way loose.

"I want you to stay," he informed her. She felt him nuzzling her neck with his nose. His hand began to explore her body once again.

"Haven't you had enough? You won the bet," she started.

"What bet," he questioned her. He was awakening her senses with his gentle touch and warm breath caressing her soft skin.

"The one with you doing what you do," she didn't want to say the whole thing.

"You mean making you have at least four orgasms?" Even though she couldn't see him, she could hear the cockiness in his voice. He had every right to sound that way. The man had her begging and damn near crying before he was finished with her. She had never experienced anything like it before in all of her years.

"Um, yeah that," she stuttered. She was glad that the lights were off because her face was on fire.

"Why are you in a rush to leave?"

"I need to go home, take a long shower, and go to bed." Her body was spent. She knew that her legs were going to be sore later on.

"You can do all of that here. Besides, I'm snug and cozy. So are you. You might as well stay and get your rest on." His logic did make sense. She was already in the bed and she was very comfortable snuggled up next to him.

"Okay, but you have to take me home in the morning." Leslie tossed out as she relaxed.

"That's fine. I can do that. Now slide on back next to me, baby." She did as she was told and they both drifted off into a deep slumber.

***

When Leslie finally did wake, the sun was pouring through the edges of the blinds and the bed was empty. She looked around the room, not sure of where she was at the moment. Then the night before came rushing to her mind along with all of the positions that Keith had her in. She took her time in appraising the room. He was nowhere in sight. She instantly began to wonder if he was regretting all that had transpired the night before. Leslie made her way to his private bathroom, glad that he had one, so she could freshen up before attempting to make her escape. She was hoping that he was gone so she wouldn't have to face him or the other guys.

After she gave herself a quick glance in the mirror, she picked up her purse and headed to the living room. Her plan was simple. She would walk out of the house, make her way to the bus stop and go home all without having to face anyone at all. As soon as she stepped foot into the living room, she heard a voice call out to her.

"Hey sleepyhead, I was wondering when you were going to join the living."

She turned toward the kitchen and what she saw made her weak in the knees. Keith was at the stove cooking, while only wearing a pair of jeans which were unbuttoned. The sight made her mouth water and her insides shiver. She finally found her voice and closed her mouth before asking, "What time is it?"

"It's almost noon." He threw over his shoulder as he turned his attention back to the stove. "I hope you are hungry."

"You're making breakfast?" Her surprise tickled him.

"Yeah, something like that," he smiled in her direction. "Grab a seat and I'll fix you a plate." She sat down at the table. The earlier thoughts of leaving vanished from her mind.

"How long have you been up?"

"Not too long," he told her as he set a cup of coffee in front of her. Everyone knew she loved her coffee. She couldn't start her day without the stuff.

"Where is everybody?" She didn't see anyone else lingering around the kitchen nor in the living room.

"Telvin is still in bed and Sam had something to do. The ladies left earlier I guess." He placed a plate full of food in front of her. Leslie didn't realized how famished she was until she got a whiff of her food. She forced herself to wait until he was seated and they had blessed the food before diving in. Leslie was surprised at how good the food was. Keith had made a breakfast skillet loaded down with potatoes, onions, bell peppers, sausage, ham, eggs, and cheese. He even had toast on the side.

"This is delicious!" She exclaimed as she took another bite.

"Thank you," he smiled. His eyes twinkled slightly and she wondered what was up with that.

"So where were you rushing off to?"

Leslie froze with the fork midways to her mouth. "I wasn't rushing off."

"Sure you were. I have done it plenty of times to know it when I see it," his smirk did nothing to calm her nerves.

"I was on my way home."

"How were you planning on getting there?"

"The bus," she said.

"You'd rather ride the bus instead of me taking you home?" He questioned her.

"I didn't see you. I assumed that you had other things to do."

"I told you that I would take you home and I meant it. Whenever you are ready, we can leave, but not before you finish your breakfast. I'm sure you are going to need your energy later on." Leslie didn't catch on to his meaning. In fact, she let the whole thing slip past her. After they were done eating and the dishes were cleaned, Keith went to grab a shirt and some shoes. True to his word, he drove Leslie home and walked her to the door of her apartment.

"Thanks for the ride," she said to him as she unlocked her door. Instead of replying, he walked on in behind her and closed the door. She was shocked by his actions, but what he did next left her speechless. Keith turned her around so that her back was against the door. He looked deep into her eyes before swooping down to taste her lips. His tongue invaded her mouth and she allowed it. Her defenses were weakened already.

"I want more, Leslie. I need more," he demanded. She couldn't fight him nor could she resist what he was doing to her. He released her mouth and led her to the bedroom.

"Keith, I know we…" was all she managed to get out before he ravished her mouth again. His kisses were greedy and she fed his need.

"Can I have more, baby?" He asked while his hands roamed over her body, settling in on her ass.

"Yes," she also wanted more. The man knew how to please a woman and she wanted to be pleased thoroughly again and again, over and over until she couldn't walk.
***

It was Sunday afternoon before Keith finally left her apartment. Even though he kept her very satisfied, she was glad when he exited her finally. Leslie didn't think her body could take anymore. She was still in awe of the way he was so in tune with her body. Even if she thought she didn't want sex, all he had to do was touch her in a certain way and her body came alive. Every inch of her body ached in some form or fashion. She crawled out of bed and went to the bathroom to run a bath. She eased into the hot water and let it soothe her aching muscles. Her mind replayed the weekend over and over again.

She was still amazed by the way he knew each and every one of her spots and the way he took his time in pleasing her. He made sure that she had an orgasm each and every time he took the liberty to explore her body. His touch created feelings she didn't know she possessed. He had her mind gone while pushing her to the limits of extreme pleasure. She grimaced at the thought of the not so great experiences in her past. Keith had awakened something deep within her body. Leslie knew that she would no longer settle for less than she deserved in the bedroom and she had him to thank for it. She shook her head at all of the bullshit partners to have crossed her path in the past.

What she should have done was be more vocal and express to them the type of things she liked and maybe then it might have been a good experience to add to her journal instead of all the negative crap that was already there. She busied herself with cleaning and getting prepared for the week ahead. With her music loud and a pep in her step, she made light work of her chores. Staying busy helped to distract her from replaying the events in her mind. She still couldn't believe all that transpired over the course of two days. She finished her rounds and braced herself for the inquisition she knew was coming her way via her best friend, Darcy. There was no way in hell Darcy would allow her to keep quiet about him and their time spent together. She would pry and pry until she found out every little sordid detail.

Chapter 4

Leslie was relaxing on the couch reading Anna Black's, "Now You Wanna Come Back," when she heard a knock on the door. Her eyes rolled back in her head as she got up from her spot. Knowing it was Darcy; she opened the door and went back to her seat and picked up her book.

"Um, Miss Thang, spill it." Darcy didn't waste any time with greetings. She wanted to know details. Leslie knew she had to give Darcy something to get her off of her back for the time being. She closed her book and placed it on the end table. Darcy was not about to let her finish reading at this rate and she knew it.

"Spill what? You already know what happened," she blushed. Darcy was demanding and Leslie knew it was only a matter of time before she had her spilling her gust. They'd shared mostly everything over the years and she knew this time would be no different, except she'd probably not go into too many details being that Darcy was Keith's first cousin.

"Oh no, don't try that crap with me. Come on now, did he win? I imagine that he did if you guys spent another night together."

"And how do you know that?" Leslie asked her. She hadn't told anyone about that just yet. Her friend always managed to surprise her with all of the shit she found out about that had absolutely nothing at all to do with her. Nosy is what Leslie often referred to her friend as.

"Girl please, don't forget that he is my cousin. Plus, I drove by here a couple of times and I saw his car out front each time." Darcy raised an expertly arched eyebrow at her. She was more than ready for the juicy gossip that was about to be revealed.

"You were spying on me?" Leslie questioned her best friend, prolonging the inevitable.

"Hell no, I was coming to get the scoop, but the scoop was still here. So, what gives? Are you guys dating now or what?" Darcy kicked off her shoes and folded her feet beneath her on the couch.

"No, none of that, we are friends. He dared me and I accepted. He proved his point very well, over and over again. I am a believer now!" She told Darcy.

"So, he put it on you and that's all there is to it? You guys aren't going to explore other options like a relationship?"

"No, we aren't. We are good." Leslie hadn't thought about being that way with Keith. She preferred being single to being in a relationship with any guy. Darcy should know that and not expect her to change it just because a man worked her body over big time.

"Are you planning on sleeping with him again?" Darcy couldn't believe what she was hearing. She thought Keith and Leslie would make a perfect couple and she always had. She had been trying to get them together for ages.

"I'm not planning on it, but anything is possible. I would be lying if I said that I wouldn't. I am now very aware of what he is working with and if the situation arises, I'm sure that I would. I don't know about him."

"I'm positive he would too." Darcy shook her head, "I can't believe you guys did it! Wow, my best friend and my cousin! We are practically family now." She exclaimed as she clapped her hands.

"Chill out girlfriend, it was just sex. Dang, you are acting like we are getting married or something."

"You never know," she said with a wink.

"Whatever. Do you want a glass of wine?" She asked her friend as she made her way to the kitchen.
"It took you long enough to ask," Darcy rolled her eyes at Leslie. "Oh and by the way, I know you gonna let me borrow that book when you are done."

"Not if you don't leave me alone. And guess what? The shit is good too." Leslie goaded Darcy with her book. She knew that Anna Black was Darcy's favorite author of all times.

"Whatever, okay I'll leave you alone for now, but I want that book by the end of the week." Darcy didn't play when it came to reading. She was just as much of a bookworm as Leslie. That was probably one of the reasons they bonded so well in their younger days. They'd always shared their mutual love of books. The conversation finally switched and Leslie was more than happy for the change. The two discussed the last book that was assigned to their book club.

With the bottle of wine depleted and Darcy long gone, Leslie crawled into bed and fell into a much needed, deep sleep.

Chapter 5

Keith hadn't really seen much of Leslie in the past three weeks even though she was a permanent fixture in his mind. Hardly a day passed without some random thought of her filling his head, making him want to call her up and beg for a date. He held fast and kept his pride intact. He knew that if he gave in in the slightest form, he would be a goner for sure. With the year heading on its way out, he knew he would be spending a lot more time around her since the group of friends normally saw one another throughout the remaining holidays.

Fall was creeping in and he wanted some warm thighs around his waist. Not just any thighs at that. They needed to be attached to a beautiful lady with a head full of wild curls and soft pouty lips that he craved on a daily basis. He had spoken to her on the phone and sent her a couple of text messages. He was glad that she didn't turn out to be one of those clingy women that would automatically assume that after their weekend together they would be in a relationship by now. Instead, she responded like she always did and that was fine with him. Well, it was up until he saw her enter the club. The friends had all agreed to meet up at Club Virgo to celebrate Bre's birthday. She had just joined the 30's club and she was letting her hair down and saying goodbye to her 20's. Keith's eyes were glued to Leslie as she danced with her friends. The short, spaghetti strapped, gold dress she had on left little to the imagination. His gazed wandered to her breasts and he recalled the way she responded to him when he took her nipples into his mouth. Her breasts were so sensitive that she would sometimes orgasm just with him sucking on her nipples and he loved the hell out of that shit. Leslie had been on his mind heavily and he needed to rectify the situation soon. He saw a guy approach her and start to make conversation. Leslie smiled at the man and let him take her hand and pull her towards the bar. Keith felt a stab of jealousy in his gut. The feeling surprised the hell out of him. Telvin caught him staring and he elbowed him in the side. "Man, what's up with that look?"

"Nothing," he mumbled turning his attention away from Leslie. Attempting to keep his true feelings on the low, he picked up his drink and took a swig after responding to his friend. He wasn't interested in going into details about his and Leslie's relationship or whatever it was they were doing with one another.

"Yeah, tell me anything, but your look says it all."

"What does my look say?" He looked at Telvin in disbelief, waiting for him to toss out some random bull.

"It's telling me that you want Leslie. It's telling me that you are scoping out the competition." Telvin was on point with his observation. He was always on top of his game. Keith could never manage to get anything past him with his nosy ass.

"You think he is competition for a man like me," Keith scoffed, "because I don't think so. I promise you that he isn't getting any of that, not tonight, not any other night for that matter."

"Oh, confident, are we?" Sam interjected, jumping in the conversation. It wasn't often they had the chance to pick on Keith. Usually he was always straight laced and kept things in line.

"Yeah I am. She knows what's up with me. She would have to learn with him. It would be like a guessing game. Trying to guess if he will be worth it, whereas with me, she already knows." Keith took a sip of his drink and turned his attention back to Leslie. They had moved back to the dance floor. She was moving her body provocatively and the guy was mesmerized by it. Keith saw him watching her butt and licking his lips. He was overcome with the desire to smash the guy's face in.

Leslie came back to the table with a big smile on her face. She slid in her seat and took a big drink of water before glancing around the table at her friends.

Darcy was the first to strike up the conversation, "Dang Leslie, I haven't seen you dance that much in a few years, not since college really."

"I know right. Girl, I'm planning on working that dance floor all night." Leslie said as she fanned her face.

"And that guy too?" Bre asked her slyly.

"Yes, possibly him too," she smiled shyly at her friends. "He does have some nice moves. He might be working with something in the bedroom." Keith ignored the look Darcy threw at him. He was not about to let her give all of that sweetness to another man while he was right there at the table with her.

"He might be working with something, but you won't be finding out anything about that tonight," he informed her. A hush fell over the table as all eyes flew to Leslie.

"What are you talking about?"

"I'm talking about the fact that you will not be giving it up to him tonight." He looked her in the eyes as he spoke.

"How do you know that? If I want to, then I will." She challenged him with her words and her eyes.

"I know because you will be giving it to me tonight," he stated all matter-of-factually. His confidence was making Leslie feel some type of way and he knew it. She was always easy for him to read.

"How do you figure that?" Her eyes challenged him to say exactly what it was that was on his mind.

"I know you enjoyed our time together just as much as I did. I want more and so do you and I want it tonight. He can't have it, not tonight, not ever really." He let his statement hang in the air for a moment before sitting back in his chair. She was stunned, he could tell, but there was no way he was going to let her go home alone or with someone other than him. There was no way he'd back down now. It was out there in the open, if she knew him like he knew her, then she'd know he was dead ass serious.

38

"Damn cuz, it's like that?" Darcy said, attempting to lighten the mood at the table. They were all curious as to which one would come out on top, literally.

"I'm just stating facts," he said while still watching Leslie fidgeting in her seat. He knew she was recalling the way he stroked her body. At that moment, the guy in question approached the table and asked Leslie if she wanted to dance again. She took his hand and looked back at Keith, "Don't you think I would have to be in agreement with your plans, which I am not," she said as the guy began to pull her out on the floor. He watched her hips sway as she walked to the dance floor. His hands itched to touch her there.

"My man, Keith, you win some you lose some. And from the looks of it, you just lost that round." Sam chided him.

"I didn't lose yet and I won't be losing at all. Mark my words, she will be leaving with me tonight and that is a promise." He told them, never taking his eyes off of her. She looked back at the table and her gazed found his. He held it for a while then he finished his drink, stood up from the table, and walked to the dance floor to claim his lady. He made his way to her and politely pulled her to him then turned to the guy and asked, "May I have a few dances with this lovely lady?" The man looked as if he was going to object. Keith did not give him the chance to voice it. He calmly steered her in a different direction and started dancing with her.

"That was rude," she pouted as his eyes took in her full luscious lips.

"No, it wasn't. I asked him first," he winked at her, trying to keep from swooping down and claiming her mouth.

"You didn't give him a chance to answer your question." She informed him as their bodies melted together.

"I don't need his permission to dance with you. He's the one that needs mine. I was your friend first. Friends always come before strangers, you know that."

She conceded to him, "Okay, let me see what you got then." And for the next hour they tore the dance floor up. Keith would have been happy to continue but Leslie begged for a break. She told him that her feet were killing her. He could imagine with those sky high heels she had on. Sam was the only one left at the table when they got there.

"Why aren't you out there cutting a rug on the dance floor?" Leslie asked him while Keith ordered them drinks.

"Girl you know I got two left feet. I only dance in the bedroom." He said to her.

"Oh TMI for me," she laughed while fanning herself with her napkin. Keith noticed how her face lit up when she smiled. He had always thought she was pretty, but tonight she was down right gorgeous. In his mind, she was by far the most beautiful woman in the club that night. He pulled his chair closer to hers and whispered in her ear, "What about me?"

"Meaning," she turned towards him.

"Do you want to see my moves in the bedroom?" His hand caressed her thigh beneath the table.

"I have already seen them." Playing hard to get, she rolled her eyes at him. That made his dick jump at the challenge.

"Not all of them," his hand went higher up her thigh. There were plenty of things he wanted to show her; different ways he intending on stroking her kitty. He just had to get her to loosen up a little because he didn't want to scare her with his inner freak.

"Oh no," she wouldn't look at him as she spoke so he took her chin and turned her face to his.

"No! I have more that I can show you. That is if you are willing to forget about that dude and go home with me instead."

"I don't want to go home with you." She told him without hesitation. Keith's mind was working overtime trying to come up with a plan to have his way with her when she eased his mind.

"I'd rather us go to my place. We won't have to worry about being too loud or any interruptions." She looked up at him with a little smile on her lips. His heart thudded in his chest. He couldn't wait to get her all alone.

"Can we leave now?" He knew that he was being greedy, but damn, he wanted like hell to be inside of her body. She ran her fingers down his jaw line and placed a small kiss on his lips.

"I don't think Bre would be too happy with that. We are here for her, remember," she said against his mouth. He deepened the kiss and when she tried to pull away, he held her in place until he was finished. He knew that she could see the desire all over his face and he didn't care, not one little bit. He wanted her and that was all there was to it.

"I think she would be okay with us leaving," Keith was sure of it. Bre had been hinting around for the last few weeks about him hooking back up with Leslie. Now he was taking her advice.

"What about…," she started to say but Keith swallowed the rest of her words with his mouth. He nibbled on her bottom lip, begging for entrance. Once she allowed him to explore, he heard blood rushing by his ears. He deepened the kiss and his tongue danced with hers. His heartbeat sped up when her tongue slipped past his lips. He was a goner and there wasn't shit he could do about it.

"How do you expect me to ask you anything if you won't let me get it out?" she asked him once he ended the kiss.

"You don't need to ask me anything. You only need to answer me, okay." He was running his fingers through her hair. "Can we leave right now, Leslie?"

"Yes," she answered finally and he felt like jumping for joy. He had forgotten all about Sam sitting at the table with them. He glanced at his friend with a look of embarrassment on his face. Sam smiled a knowing smile at him. "I guess I will see you Monday evening after work."

"Yeah whatever," he told Sam.

"I'm just saying, the last time you were gone for the whole weekend." He laughed at Keith's expression. Keith looked over at Leslie hopping that she was not listening to Sam. To his delight she wasn't. She was busy scanning the club for Bre and Darcy and she missed the whole exchange. Keith threw Sam a "Shut the hell up" look before helping Leslie to her feet.

"I need to tell them we are leaving," she said as she walked over to the spot they were dancing in. Keith followed closely behind her. He didn't want any of the other men stepping on his plans for her. He made eye contact with the guy from earlier, he looked pissed. Keith gave a shrug and placed his arm protectively around her waist. He was making it obviously clear to the man that he was familiar with her and that he was the one going home with her. When they reached their friends, Leslie informed them that they were leaving.

Darcy gave her a kiss on the check and Keith a hug. Before releasing him she warned him, "Don't hurt her." He nodded his head at her. She needn't worry because Leslie would be in good hands, his hands all night long. Possibly all weekend long if she agreed with him and allowed him to stay that long. She agreed and he stayed. He enjoyed being with her like that in the privacy of her home. They spent the time talking and watching movies. He hadn't felt so at ease in a very long time. Leslie was a beautiful woman inside and out. He found himself wanting to spend more and more time with her. Instead of acting on it, he continued on with their friendship even though he wanted more. He wanted her to be his and his only.

But she was the type of woman that wouldn't take too kindly to his domineering ways he figured. The way he'd been feeling lately was a shock to his system. He was all for relationships and romance and all. It just wasn't in his cards, well it wasn't until Leslie managed to slide under his armor and worm her way into his heart without even trying to. Yes, he had to come up with a plan to make her see that what they had was more than sex; what they had was worth exploring.

Chapter 6

"What are your plans for tomorrow?" Keith asked her while stroking her back. He was working out the knots that she had. He had managed to convince her to let him stay another night in her bed. The time they shared was the most relaxing he'd been in a long time and his thoughts were taking on a life of their own, leading him down a slippery slope.

"I have church in the morning then lunch at my grandmother's house." She leaned back into his touch, relaxing even more with sleep only an inch away.

"Oh yeah, what is she cooking up?" Leslie knew his stomach always ruled his decisions when choosing where to go. He had to make sure he was going to get his eat on at some point in time during the outings that he went to. It was amazing the way his body was rock solid without an ounce of fat with the way he put away food. She assumed that all of those rough basketball games helped with keeping his body intact. Whatever it was was definitely paying off in his favor.

"I don't know," She looked up at him and asked, "Do you want to go with me?"

"You mean to your grandmother's house?" He raised an eyebrow at her.

"Both, to church and to her house," she was expecting him to say no, but to her surprise he agreed to accompany her to both places the next day. She snuggled up closer to him and drifted off into a land of dreams.

True to his word, he went to the morning service with her and enjoyed himself. They also had a wonderful time with her family. He wasn't a stranger. In fact, he fitted right in with the rest of the men. The men were all in the living room watching a game while the ladies were in the kitchen/dining room running their mouths and putting the finishing touches on the dinner. Leslie's grandmother placed a wrinkled weathered hand on top of hers.

"Keith is a lovely young man. I'm glad he is your friend. Although I am beginning to suspect there is more to it than that. You two seem a little closer than before. Is there a chance there's a relationship in the works for the two of you?"

"We are just friends." Leslie blushed. She despised fibbing to the older woman, but she knew if she let on that things between her and Keith were quickly turning into something else, her grandmother would be on the way to planning their wedding. So she did the only thing she figured to work, deny it. Well, at least until she was sure of Keith's intentions.

"You say that, but the way he watches you tells a whole different story. He doesn't like you being out of his sight for too long." Her grandmother winked at her again and smiled. The woman saw through everything, Leslie thought to herself.

"Big Mama, he is just being nice and that's all." Leslie lowered her head hoping no one paid attention to her flaming cheeks. She had to learn how to get that under control, the blushing and all.

"Yeah, tell an old woman anything. Just remember that I have been around the block a time or two and I know a few things. And one of those things that I know is the look of love on a person's face. You both have it. For goodness sake, he came to church with you. That in itself speaks volumes because he doesn't go to church on a regular basis."

"Okay, you are right. I like him a lot. This is all still new and I don't want to rush it," she confessed to the older woman. Her grandmother had always been her voice of reasoning in her time of confusions.

"Honey, don't worry about a thing. If he is the one, you will know it. If he is the one, he will let you know. When the time is right all will be revealed and you will no longer have to wonder where his heart lies." Her grandmother spoke her words of wisdom in a slight whisper to keep the other women from eavesdropping on their conversation. Leslie gave her grandmother a tight hug before checking to see if Keith was okay.

She found him in the den with the rest of the men watching a game on her grandfather's 50inch plasma television that all of his grandchildren had gotten him for

Christmas. It was his pride and joy as he often told them all. She made her way over to where Keith was sitting.

"Are you okay? I mean do you want anything to drink?" She stammered on. The conversation with her grandmother had left her with a bundle nervous.

"I'm fine, though I would enjoy some company." He told her with a sly look on his face. Even though Keith was used to being around the Adams family, he craved her closeness. He often stopped by to check on her mother and her grandparents. He'd even been to quite a few cookouts before. Things were a little different now since he and Leslie were working on building a relationship.

"You are in the company of all the guys but you're still feeling lonely? Explain to me how that works please?"

Keith pulled her down on his lap and wrapped his arms around her. Once she found a comfortable spot, he leaned his mouth to her ear and whispered, "I'd rather be in the presence of you and your delicious body. I'd rather be stroking you, tasting you." Leslie knew if her skin was brighter, everyone would have noticed her blushing.

"You can't say things like that in my gram's house. She can hear you," she warned him. She could tell he wasn't buying it. The look of disbelief on his face made her smile. "I'm serious, Keith, that woman hears and sees all." Keith was getting ready to respond when Leslie's grandmother's voice caught his attention.

"She's right you know. I do hear and see everything. Especially when all of y'all are trying to sneak and get away with something. I don't understand why you fail to remember that detail, Keith." She winked her eye at him before handing her husband a bottle of Bud Light.

"I told you," Leslie smiled at him.

"How does she always do that?" He was amazed that the old lady had actually heard their conversation.

"Oh I have my ways. If you plan on being in this family, you will get used to it eventually." She said to Keith while leaving the room. He looked to Leslie and shook his head. "Wow, I bet you guys couldn't get away with anything when you guys were growing up?"

"Oh no, not at all, and we all learned that lying to her was pointless." She chuckled as she thought about the times she tried to put one over on her grandmother.

"Well, I guess we will have to make sure our children know the deal."

"Our children," the question was evident in her eyes. He seemed to want more than what he let on. She was sort of afraid to hope for more. She wasn't interested in being hurt.

Keith ran the back of his hand along her cheek, "Yes, our children. I hope you don't think I have any intentions of ever letting you go. Naw, I have to keep you for mine." Leslie's hand came up and closed around his before pulling it to her mouth and placing a kiss on it.

"That sounds absolutely marvelous." Her smile showed as bright as the sun. She placed a small kiss on the corner of his mouth before returning to the kitchen to be interrogated by the others.

It was well into the night before they managed to leave each loaded with plates piled high by her grandmother. That night Leslie asked and he stayed. That night they slow danced and held one another close. They talked, really talked about what is was that they both wanted out of life and they explored one another's mind as well as body.

Chapter 7

October 2009

"Now will you please tell me what is going on with you and Keith?" Bre asked her one night when it was just the three of them. The three women were having a movie night at Leslie's apartment and Keith had just called her. She knew that answering right then was not in her best interest. So, she let it go to voicemail and made a mental note to return his call after the girls left. Thanksgiving was right around the corner and she knew that he probably wanted to see what she had going on for the holidays.

All she wanted to do was spend it at home and possibly invite him over. Working in the call center was beginning to gyrate her nerves. Keith was her escape from the crazy world of complaining customers. He knew how to erase all of the drama she'd experienced in a day with those sweet kisses of his that she adored so much.

"Nothing, we are just friends," she said. She wasn't ready to admit to anyone just yet about their progress and her true feelings for him. She wanted to hold on to their privacy a tad bit longer. She knew she had her friends' trust and well-wishes. She just didn't want to share what she and Keith had with anyone just yet.

"Just friends my ass," Darcy threw in. "I don't want to hear that. You don't sex your friends the way you been giving it up to him."

"You don't know that!" Leslie argued, but she knew it was a weak one. She had been spending a lot of time with Keith. Any time they did things as a group; Keith would always be by her side or pay for her, even hold her hand at times. And he'd always end up going home with her.

"Look, we know you giving up the booty! Hell it must be good because he hasn't mentioned another woman in a while. Plus, he always has that silly ass smile on his face." Bre said.

"He sure does and so do you," Darcy agreed with her.

"I do not. Y'all are just being nosy" Leslie was trying to keep herself from blushing, that's all her girlfriends would need to see.

"That too," Darcy admitted. "I think it's cute, but you guys need to stop acting like y'all don't want a relationship. It is practically one now."

"No it isn't. We only hook up every now and again. It is like a stress reliever for us both." She felt her face flaming and knew her friends were enjoying her embarrassment.

"I'm guessing a damn good stress reliever because you guys are always together. I mean shit, the man went to church with you," Bre interjected while Darcy burst out laughing.

"You guys are so wrong for being all up in my business like that." Leslie fanned her face, hoping to cool off a little before she actually starts sweating.

"You are wrong for trying to pretend that you don't have feeling for Keith and all of that shit. We can read your ass like a book and you know it, so tell the damn truth for once in your life." Darcy threw out before pouring herself another glass of wine. Since it was Bre's night to drive, Darcy was free to indulge a lot.

"Of course I do. He's my friend just like you guys are my friends. And don't trip, I always tell the truth home girl."

"But we ain't stroking that kitty on a regular basis." Darcy told her. Bre fell over laughing and clutching her side. Leslie shook her head and thought to herself, if they only knew the things he and I really did talk about they would never let me rest.

"Keith and I are good. Neither one of us is interested in being tied down. This right here works for us both without the extra pressure of being in a relationship." She preached to her girlfriends. Keith chose that moment to call her back. This time she answered, not concerned with what her friends thought any longer.

"Hello," she said into the phone.

"Hey babe, how are you?" she loved the sound of his deep voice. It sent chills down her spine every time he spoke.

"I'm great. How are you?" She couldn't keep the smile from her face and her nosy ass friends were all in her business.

"I'm good, but I could be better." He told her point blank.

"How so?"

"I could be great, better than great actually. That is if my babe wants some company tonight." Keith told her. She heard the plea in his words.

"I already have company," she informed him. She intentionally forgot to mention that it was her girlfriends.

"Oh yeah, who?" Keith asked her trying to keep the jealousy out of his voice. He did a lousy job of it though because Leslie smiled to herself.

"No one important,"

"If they aren't important then you wouldn't mind telling me. I mean I just want to make sure my special lady is in good company, that's all." Keith reasoned with her.

"Oh it is good company, great company really." She was having fun with this. Bre and Darcy had stopped watching the movie so that they could pay attention to her conversation. She ignored their stares and continued on.

"Babe don't tease,"

"I'm not." She wanted him to come over but their little game was fun to her.

"Well, let me come and see you?" His tone was low and seductive. There was no way he was letting her get out of allowing him to come over. The more he spoke, the wetter she became.

"But I told you that I have company," she whined into the phone.

"So what, I don't care about that. I just need to see you." Keith wasn't giving up and she was thrilled. She hadn't seen him in almost a week. It was time for a tune-up on her kitty. Her friends had gathered around her listening intently to her side of the conversation.

"You only want to lay eyes on me?" She teased him.

"No, but if that's all I can get, then, yes that's all."

"Okay, you can come over, but don't be expecting anything," she warned Keith knowing full well that she was on the verge of kicking her friends out before he even arrived.

"Alright, I'll be there in a minute. See you in a little bit babes,"

"Okay," she hung up the phone and noticed that Bre and Darcy had big smiles on their faces.

"What?" She asked them as they peered at her with looks of the Cheshire cat. She shook her head at the nosy pair. They wouldn't keep letting her slide without giving them some juice regarding her relationship with Keith.

"You know what!" Darcy exclaimed while Bre added her two cents.

"Leslie, oh my goodness, you guys are a couple!" She said while holding her heart.

"I wish you guys would stop saying that." Even though she was acting like it would be a normal visit, she ran to the bathroom to check on her appearance. They didn't have to know that every time she saw him her heart skipped a beat. When she was finished she went back to the living room to be bombarded with questions from the ladies. Before she had a chance to answer the doorbell ranged. She ran to the door while Bre and Darcy looked at one another with shock on their faces. She opened the door and waved him in. As soon as he crossed over the threshold, he pulled her to him and planted an open mouth kiss on her lips. His arms felt like instant heaven to her and she melted on the spot.

"I thought you said that you only wanted to see me," she said breathlessly after he released her.

"I never said "only" Leslie." He joked with her. "Where is your company?"

"Right here, cuz." Darcy called out to him from the living room. Keith walked on in and closed the door behind him. He looked to Bre then Darcy and back to Leslie. She couldn't stop the grin from taking over her face.

"I told you I had company," she gloated.

"Yeah, but you didn't say who," he wrapped his arms around her waist and whispered in her ear, "You know that I'm going to punish you for that right?"

"Why?" she pretended to pout and he gave her ass a smack.

"I raced over here thinking that I was going to find some dude all sprawled out on the couch making moves on my lady." He said his lady and she caught it and held on to it for dear life. She wanted to say something, but not in the presence of others. This was a conversation best held between the two of them without the opinion of others.

"So Keith, what are you doing out at this time? Don't you have to work in the morning?" Darcy probed.

"Yes, I do. You do too, right? So don't you think you should be heading home to get your much needed beauty rest," he teased her relentlessly.

"Maybe you should too. I mean we don't want you to be grumpy at work."

"Oh I definitely won't be that."

"I don't think you should have that beer. You have to drive home and you know how I feel about drinking and driving." Darcy preached on. Leslie knew what she was up to. She shook her head and watched the scene unfold.

"I'll only have one," he told her. His mind was in other places, preferably in bed with his head buried deep between Leslie's thighs.

"Yeah, you say that now. You know your butt should be in the bed gearing up for that big day tomorrow," she went on and on.

"If you and Bre go ahead and leave, then I can go to bed!" That shut both of them up real quick. Leslie slapped him on the arm and told him to quit being mean to her company.

"Damn Leslie, he must want in your panties very badly." Bre coughed into her hand.

"Bre," Leslie cried out. She was beyond embarrassed.

"What? You know he does, stop fronting."

"Come on, girl. Let's go and let these two get to knocking boots before Keith throws us out." Darcy joked with Bre and she laughed. On the way out of the door, Bre turned to Leslie and called out, "Have fun and bust a nut for me!" Then she closed the door before Leslie could even utter a word.

"About time," Keith mentioned to no one in particular as he started removing her clothes. His hands felt wonderful on her skin. "I've been craving you all week, Leslie, my love."

"Why did it take you so long to call me?" she asked him as she ripped off his shirt. Her mouth found its way to his now exposed chest.

"I didn't want to bug you, baby." He moaned as her lips wrapped around his nipple. She raked her nails down his chest.

"You do plenty of things to me, but bugging me is not one of them," she admitted to him.

"Why don't you tell me what all I do to you?" He ran his hands up and down her arms. She loved the feel of his rough hands on her soft skin.

"How about if I show you instead," she flirted with him.

"Show me then Leslie," Keith was hard as a rock and she was ready to blow his mind.

She took his hand and guided him to her bedroom for a night of exquisite pleasure. For the first time since they had become intimate, he let her take the lead and show him what she had on her mind. The things she did to his body left him speechless. His mind was reeling from the mind blowing nuts she gave him over and over. After the last one, he rolled over onto his back and pulled her close to him before falling into a deep peaceful slumber.

Chapter 8

Keith could no longer claim the single status. He was head over heels in love with Leslie and he didn't care if the whole world knew it. He wanted them to take their relationship to the next level. Marriage and children plagued his dreams. Leslie was his crown jewel, his queen. Two months of dating and he already knew he was done for. He spent more time at her place than he did his own. His boys were constantly teasing him about paying rent in a place that he was hardly at which was real talk. That convinced him to speak with her about them living together.

She was nervous at first, but she gave in and agreed that it would be for the best. Leslie was cleaning the kitchen after serving him a scrumptious breakfast when he made up his mind to make his move.

"Hey baby, I was thinking that we should make this permanent." He said to her while looking through the newspaper.

She turned towards him, "Make what permanent?" Her mind was on the dishes. She was totally unaware of his intentions he could tell as much.

"You and I, we should make our relationship permanent." He glanced up and caught her look. His eyes held hers as realization dawned in her hazel eyes. He loved staring in her almond shaped eyes while making love to her. He felt himself stirring so he switched his thoughts back to the matter at hand.

"What are you saying, Keith?" Complete shock was written on her face.

He walked around the island, got down on one knee and pulled the small black box from his pocket. "I simply adore you, my beautiful Leslie. You are always in my thoughts; from the moment I awake until I close my eyes and drift off to sleep. I want to spend the rest of my life waking up next to you, loving you, holding you, catering to your each and every wish. Please be mine for eternity." He took the ring from the box and placed it upon her shaking hand. His heart was pounding as he waited for her answer.

"Keith, I…." she stammered. A moment of panic entered his heart. He hadn't thought about the possibility of her saying no. He assumed she felt the same as he did. As the seconds ticked by, doubt began to enter his mind. Rejection was making its way into his mind and heart.

"Before you answer, think about it for a little bit, maybe a few days. I can wait for you," he told her while attempting to control the quiver in his voice while the thump in his chest increased. He was sure she could hear it beating if she listened closely.

"I don't need to think about. You caught me by surprise that's all." She said to him while her hand caressed his cheek. Without thinking about it, he leaned in to her touch.

"Oh," he waited for her to go on with hope blossoming in his heart.

"My answer is yes. Yes, I will marry you," she cried as tears spilled down her face. A face that he adored. He stood and pulled her to him. She fit into his arms oh so perfectly. Her body melted into his just like a piece to a puzzle. They completed one another on so many levels. His Leslie; his love.

"Mine forever," he whispered in her ear as they held onto one another. He wanted to yell to the world that she said yes. He squeezed her a little more, not willing to release her anytime soon. Right here in his arms is where he felt that she'd always belong and that's where he planned to keep her for the rest of their days.

***

Keith adored his Leslie and she craved her Keith. Their relationship was ideal, exactly what each wanted in a partner. Instead of broadcasting their relationship to the masses, they decided to keep it amongst themselves for a while. Privacy was the way they chose to proceed. Working on getting to know one another in that way without the outside world influencing them had a delightful twang to it. Throughout the work days, Leslie carried a smile more often than not. A smile that said, "I have a secret and it's freaking awesome." Things were moving along accordingly. They slipped into a daily routine of life and it was great for them. As time progressed, one would hardly ever catch one without the other aside from work. He preferred having his lady, his love, right by his side at all times. He probably would have her at work with him if it was allowed to happen. But then if he did that, he knew he wouldn't be able to get any work done because he would have her spread out on his desk for most of the day without a doubt.

So he resisted temptation and went to work alone, counting the hours until quitting time, until Leslie time began.

Chapter 9

Leslie was more than a little nervous as hell upon leaving the doctor's office. She was indeed carrying Keith's child and she wasn't sure how he would react to the news. She knew he loved her, but they really hadn't discussed when they would start their family. They hadn't even set a date for the wedding as of yet. She wiped her eyes for the millionth time and shook off the doubt clouding what was supposed to be a moment of happiness. She'd always wanted to be a mother and now her dreams were coming true. Regardless of Keith's reaction, she would love and care for her baby to the best of her abilities.

She jumped into her Tracker and headed to the gym to clear her mind. Working out had become a great way to clear her head when her thoughts were overwhelming. Plus, it made her body nice and tight for her man! After a quick workout, she swam a couple of laps to cool off before heading home. Keith wouldn't be over until around seven that night. That gave her plenty of time to think of a way to break the news to him. Even though she wanted to call and tell her girls, she knew it would be best if she let him know first.

"Hey baby, where are you?" Keith called out from the living room. He no longer knocked before entering. Instead he used his key, the key that he'd had for a while. They had all exchanged keys in case of one of them ever losing theirs.

"I'm in the bedroom," she answered. She was attempting to rearrange her closet. It was time for her to get rid of some of the crap she had. Plus, she had needed to focus her attention on something else before she drove herself crazy wondering how he would respond to the news.

"Damn baby, you think you have enough clothes?" He glanced around the closet taking in the scene before him.

"I know and I'm trying to get rid of some. It's too much clutter in here." She said to him while placing her hands on her hips and surveying her walk-in closet. She really did need to stop buying clothes. Her ultimate weakness was sales and consignment shops. She was a sucker for a good bargain even if she didn't need it. She often told herself that eventually an occasion would arise for her to make use of an item.

"Why don't you take a break," he said, walking up behind her and wrapping his arms around her waist. She leaned back into him and suddenly cleaning the closet was no longer important to her.

"I could use one. Besides, I'm kind of hungry now." She hadn't eaten that much and she knew that would have to change, especially with her eating for two now.

"How about if I take my favorite lady out for dinner," He kissed the back of her neck and waited for her reply.

"That would be nice. Where are we going?"

"Your choice, love."

"Can we get Chinese? I have a taste for some chow mien and pot stickers." Her excitement was evident.

"You can have whatever you want. Come on let's go get some grub." He led her from the closet and into the living room to gather their things before heading out to his car.

All through dinner, she contemplated on how to tell him about the baby. Instead of waiting and hoping for the perfect moment, she blurted it out when dinner was almost over.

"Keith, I'm pregnant." She threw out while stuffing a chicken pot sticker in her mouth. She figured if her mouth was occupied, he wouldn't expect her to respond immediately.

He was shocked to say the least. Her heart thumped in her chest, afraid of what he may say. All of it was for naught because a huge grin adorned his face. "I'm going to be a dad?" he asked, confirming what she'd already said.

She finally smiled at him. "Yes, you are."

"Wow, I can't believe it, I mean, when? How far along are you?" His words were stumbling over one another. She laughed at him.

"About three months as far as I know, after I have an ultrasound there will be a more specific time frame." She relayed to him what her doctor had told her earlier that day.

"When will we have to go for that?"

"In a few weeks, you don't have to go though."

"Oh no, I'm going. I want to be there every step of the way right with you, love." He pulled her hand to his lips and kissed her palm. "I love you, Leslie."

"I love you too, Keith." She brightly smiled at him. They finished their dinner in record time, anxious to get home.

Chapter 10

December 2009

Christmas was quickly approaching and Leslie was excited to be sharing her favorite holiday with Keith. This was the first time ever that she'd spent her holiday in a serious relationship and she was completely over the moon at the thought of doing so. She loved gift shopping. It was something about being in the mall surrounded by all of the Christmas shoppers, the decorations, and the joyful music. This year she was in search of the perfect gift for her love. They'd exchanged presents before, but only as friends. Now she was looking for something that had meaning and conveyed her feelings for him.

She was totally and completely in love with him and her gift should let him know it without her not having to use words to say it. Leslie made a date of it with Bre and Darcy so they could have lunch in the process just to catch up with them. Keith had been occupying majority of her time. Aside from work, they were always together. Not that she was complaining, not in the least, but her friends were constantly attempting to get her from underneath Keith, as they often said. They wore her out after a while. She gave in to them and committed to spending the day with them at the mall.

Saturday was a glorious day. Even though it was cold as hell, the sun was shining bright and everything looked exceptionally vivid to her. They agreed to meet around ten in the morning. She found a spot and made her way to the meeting destination. They were patiently awaiting her arrival when she'd all but figured she would be the first one there. They must have been looking forward to the outing more than she had anticipated, hence their early arrival. They all managed to clear their lists in a decent amount of time even with the mall being crowded. Leslie left Keith for last. She wanted to get her girlfriends inpute on the perfect gift for him.

"You guys have seriously got to help me pick out something for Keith. I don't have a clue what to get him."

"Get him some clothes," Bre suggested.
"No, he has enough of them. This gift has to represent my feelings for him."

"And what exactly are those feelings?" Darcy asked her with a sneaky look on her face.

"You know how I feel about him, why you trying to front?"

"Hmm, I don't think you've ever admitted to us how you really feel? Do you recall her saying something to that effect Bre? Because I damn sure don't." Darcy said while smacking her lips.

"I love him, y'all know I do, or else we wouldn't be getting married." She looked at them as if they were crazy.

"People marry for many reasons, we just wanted to make sure, and that's all." Bre told her, but she knew they were bluffing. All they wanted to hear was her gushing over him. She was trying hard not to do that most of the times. She remembered how they used to make fun of women ohhhing and awing over the men in their lives. Now, she wanted to do the same, but not if her friends were going to be poking fun at her, laughing at her expense.

"Alright, fuck it. I love the man with everything in me. He is so sweet and he completes me in ways I didn't know needed it." She placed her hand across her heart. With a dreamy expression on her face, she looked at her friends, waiting for them to light into her. To her surprise, they did the opposite.

"Girl I'm so happy for you. You guys make a perfect couple." Bre exclaimed, clapping her hands together.

"I know right, I always wondered what was taking you guys so long to realize you needed to be together." Darcy added.

"You guys aren't going to make fun of me for being all lovey dovey?" She asked them, shocked by the turn of events.

"Chile, no, I am patiently awaiting my knight in shining armor." Bre said and Darcy agreed. "If anything I'm jealous of how happy he makes you. I want someone to make me happy, make me smile all of the time, have me walking all gap leg because of him dicking me down properly." The girls fell out laughing after Bre's little sermon.

After spending most of the day searching for the perfect gift, Leslie settled on something she thought would suffice. She raced home to wrap and hide the gifts before Keith came home and caught her in the act. If she was honest, one of his gifts she'd get to enjoy right along with him. She smiled to herself as she placed the items in the hall closet behind the linens. He hardly ever went in that one particular closet, so she felt it was the safest place for the gifts. She gave herself a mental pat on her back for a job well done. The most important one of his gifts she'd get right before Christmas. There would be no way to hide it if she got it sooner. She smiled as she thought about the way he'd react when he saw his gift. She hoped he would be delighted with it.

Chapter 11

Keith invited Leslie to dine with his parents. He had already informed them of his intentions concerning them growing as a family. They were thrilled at the fact of possible grandchildren in the horizon. His mother had been on the baby mission for the last few years. Now that he was in a serious relationship, she figured it was only a matter of time before she got her wish. Little did she know she was going to be a grandma sooner than she'd originally thought it would be? His mother was always fond of Leslie, which was evident at all times. She always managed to fit in with them whenever she was around. She adored his parents as they did her. The only problem he foresaw was his mother getting upset over his choice to bring Christmas in at home with Leslie. He planned on stopping by that afternoon, but Christmas Eve till the next afternoon was going to be private time for him and Leslie; the beginning of their own personal family tradition.

"What do you think I should take over to your mom's house?" Leslie asked.

"I'm not sure. Maybe you can make a dessert," he suggested to her. His mom loved cooking and there probably was little that was needed.

"Oh, I can make tiramisu." She exclaimed, clapping her hands excitedly. He smiled in her direction. He knew how she was when it came to cooking, something like his mother.

"Definitely, you know I love that," he said, licking his lips.

"And you can't have any until we get to your parents' house." She informed him. If she wasn't careful, the whole pan would be demolished before they even left home.

"Aw, come on babe. How about you make a separate pan for me?" He pleaded with his eyes begging her at the same time.

"What shall I get in return?" She winked at him. Her mind was tittering in the gutter. Making love with Keith was one of her most favorite pastimes.

"If you do that, you can get whatever you like; whatever your heart desires."

"Ooh goodie, I have something in mind." She smiled slyly at him. Vivid images of his lips between her thighs, his tongue flickering on her clit. Yeah, she was definitely going to make him his own personal pan to enjoy.

"Aw hell, what did I get myself into?" He saw the desire in her eyes! Her pheromones were through the roof and he was in tune with her body. He was quite sure her body spoke the same language as his.

"You will definitely find out soon, but right now, I have some work to do in the kitchen. So, be a good little boy and do something constructive with your time until mommy is finished." She told him with a stern look on her face. He couldn't help but to laugh at her while thinking of a new fantasy for them to act out. One with her being the teacher and him being the bad ass student stuck in detention. He laughed to himself as he as he walked out of the kitchen and headed upstairs to take a shower. Leslie was a lot like his mother, she didn't like people all in the way while she was cooking. He decided to take his time in grooming. While in the shower, his thoughts began to play back over the last year and how things transpired with Leslie. He couldn't believe he was as happy as he was.

None of his other relationships had even scratched the surface of this one. No one held a candle to his beautiful Leslie. He fell head over heels in love with her in a matter of months. If he was really honest, he might have even had feelings for her when they were just friends. All he knew was that she was his light at the end of a dark and dank tunnel. His own vision of loveliness; his queen.

Keith could tell Leslie was nervous as soon as he pulled up in front of his parent's house. He shook his head. "Why are you looking like that? It's not like this is your first time meeting them." He said to her as he turned off engine.

"I know that but this is different." She replied. She checked her face in the mirror even though she looked perfect to him. It wouldn't do any good for him to speak on it while she was a bundle of nerves She'd probably bite his head off in return.

"Not really, you know them, they know you. What's so different?"

"I wasn't fucking you then. I wasn't carrying their grandchild then. That's what's different this time around." She told him. Her look was one of amazement. "I can't believe you don't feel the same way. I mean how often do you bring pregnant fiances home to your parents?"

"Come on, baby. You know what I meant. And as far as bringing home pregnant women, you are the first."

"And what about fiances," She glanced his way quickly before flipping the visor.

"You know you are the only one, don't trip girl." He told her while he climbed from the car and went to her side to open her door. She brushed his outstretched hand to the side and got out on her own. He groaned inwardly at the action.

"Les, baby, don't be mad at me." He begged her wishing he knew what he said that pissed her off so fast. He mentally ran through the conversation again and still coming up blank.

"Who said I was mad? You must have me confused with one of your other baby mamas." She threw in as she got the pan of dessert from the back seat. He wrapped his arms around her waist before she had the chance to object to his touch. Those pregnancy hormones were not for the faint of heart he discovered.

"You know you are my one and only. If you be a good girl, daddy will treat you to something very special once we get home." He whispered to her as his lips brushed against her neck and he felt a slight tremor roll through her body.

72

"Hmm, now you want to be all lovey since you are in trouble." She said while leaning back into his hard body making his semi hard erection stiff. He pressed himself up against her letting her see for herself where his thoughts were.

"As long as the punishment is right, I'll be that." He informed her, knowing her imagination was going to be working overtime throughout dinner.

"You make me sick," she moaned as he nipped her neck.

"I make you a lot of things and right now sick sure isn't one of them. More like wet, I'm thinking." Keith was just about to let his hands wander when he heard the front door open. Before turning to see who it was, he called out, "Hi mom."

"Hey baby, what's taking you guys so long to come in? I heard y'all pull up about five minutes ago." She called out to them. Keith chuckled as he rearranged his pants and took the pan from Leslie's hands.

"Showtime baby," He winked in her direction as he made his way to where his mother stood waiting for them. He could feel the chilled look Leslie had aimed at his retreating form. Oh yeah, they were going to have plenty of fun that night, especially now that she was heated. His little firecracker in heat, he laughed to himself. His mother bypassed him and reached out to pull Leslie in for a tight embrace.

"Honey, I haven't seen you in ages. What have you been up too?" She asked as she led them in the house. That visit cemented their relationship to his parents. They were thoroughly delighted with the news they received.

Chapter 12

Much to everyone's delight, that year the snow fell just in time for them to have a white holiday. With the weather reports and the temperature, the snow would be sticking around for a while. Leslie adored white Christmases and she'd be spending it indoors with her man. She was all for it. Keith and Leslie were seated on the floor in front of the tree listening to music and sipping spiked eggnog. The ambiance was romantic and relaxing.

"I love being with you like this." Leslie confessed to him.

"So do I," he pulled her between his legs with her back to his chest. His arms slid around her waist to rest on her stomach. She laid her head back on him.

"Um mm," she moaned.

"You good?" He asked her, his warm breath tickling her neck.

"Yes, very good." Her eyes closed momentarily as she felt her body melting into his.

"I want us to remain like this forever, baby. I've never felt as good as I do at this exact moment. It's like nothing in the world matters outside of this room." His voice held so many emotions and he was well aware of it. He needed her to understand his intentions fully. His desire to be with her was overwhelming. Loving Leslie was taking over his life in ways he couldn't begin to explain, not that he was complaining at all. She was his dream woman, his perfect match.

He thought they were good as friends. Now that they were in a relationship, it was so much better. He felt completely at ease with her on all levels. The arguments were minimal and the loving was unbelievable, more so than he could have ever imagined it would be. It surpassed all of his previous encounters ten folds. It was as if he had his on little slice of heaven on earth.

"I know exactly what you mean," she agreed.

"Do you want to open your gifts tonight?"

"No, I'd rather wait until morning. Call me old fashion, but I think it will be fun with the anticipation of waiting." Her smile was contagious as he looked at the joy on her face, the happiness in her eyes. He felt some type of way knowing that he was part of the reason for that look on her face.

"That sounds like a plan to me. I'll just hold you half of the night and make love to you the rest." He kissed her on the cheek and squeezed her a little tighter.

"Um-mm, I can hardly wait for the loving." She joked with him.

"Well, we can always switch things up and make love all night. You know I'm down for whatever. It's all good with me." He winked at her. He never tired of being inside of her delicious body. His stamina and craving for her always had him at attention. More often than not, he had to control his urges just to make sure he gave her enough time to rest.

"I think I like that plan better." She turned towards him and kissed his lips lightly. He deepened the kiss and invaded her mouth with his tongue. She tasted so sweet and when she adjusted her body, he felt her warmth. His manhood was attempting to break free of his pants. He wanted to be inside of her tight wetness and it was making Keith slowly lose control.

"Damn Leslie," he growled after coming up for air. Her lips were leaving trails of fire on his neck as he palmed her ass.

"What's wrong, baby?"
"I need to be inside of you soon or I can't be held responsible for my actions." He warned her. The ways she was moving her body against him was making it difficult for him to concentrate.

"Patience, love" she whispered as her hand slid down to his dick. The gentle strokes she gave him had him catching his breath.

"Les, I'm not gonna be able to last if you don't stop now."

"Um, I don't want you to. I want to please you, taste you all over." She told him as she kissed her way down his stomach, leaving a trail of fire in her wake. Making him lose control was one of her favorite things to do. It turned her on the way his body responded to her touch, her kisses. She was never tired of pleasing him. She released his dick and took him into her warm mouth. He inhaled sharply as she drew him in as far as she could before easing him out and licking across the head catching drops of pre-cum with her tongue.

"Ah fuck," he moaned. His hips bucked as she gripped him firmly in her hands while exploring him with her mouth. Once she set the pace, his head rolled back with his eyes closed as he gave in to her and her warm mouth. She felt powerful. She felt beautiful. She had the ability to bring this man to his knees just with her touch alone. Her confidence soared throughout her body as she gave him what his body craved and more.

Standing over him as he caught his breath, Leslie slowly removed each and every article of clothing from her body. Slowly turning with her ass facing him, she heard him gasp and she smiled.

"Damn," was all he was able to say at that moment.

"Do you like it?" she asked, still not sure if it was a good idea.

"Like it, I fucking love it. You do know what this means, right?" He asked her as his fingers traced the ink of her new tattoo of his name.

"What," she whispered.
"It means that you are mine. This ass right here belongs to me forever." He smacked her ass and laughed.

"I can deal with that," she yelped when she felt his lips on her and his tongue tracing the intricate designs of her ink.

"I love this and I love you, baby."
"I'm glad you do and I love you too, Keith."
He pulled her to his lap and showed her just how much

it turned him on and she loved each minute of it.

Keith was amazed at the way her body was changing. He still was in disbelief that he had a baby on the way. He was official the first amongst his friends to become a father and he was excited as all get out. He wanted to start buying items for the baby as soon as Leslie told him, but she made him calm down and said that it would be better to wait until the seventh month of pregnancy before shopping. Even though he was itching to purchase something, he held off and deposited the money in an account for the baby.

His Leslie's belly had started to round with their child. He loved rubbing it while lying next to her. He was anxious to feel the baby's movements. They were still indecisive about names and had narrowed it down to a few possibilities. Keith convinced Leslie that they should start looking at houses for their future family. His argument was that they were already practically living together and instead of paying rent, they could be making mortgage payments on a house for their family. It made sense to her and she agreed with his plan to start house hunting.

Chapter 13

L ooking at houses with Leslie was a lot more fun than hanging out at the bar with his boys, Keith thought to himself as they left another house. With her sexual appetite nowadays, he could just about get it anywhere and anytime he wanted it. Sneaking in a corner of an empty house while the Realtor was in a different place tickled her fancy. She loved the risk and it made her orgasms that much stronger. Keith was more than happy to oblige her each and every fantasy. Even though the sex was wonderful, they were actually in the market for a home. He wanted them to be settled before their child was born.

They both were saving for their future home. The process of actually picking out a house was beginning to get on Leslie's nerves. She was more than convinced they wouldn't be able to find a place before the baby arrived. She wanted everything situated and ready. Keith promised her that eventually one would appeal to her when she least expected it to. That worked for a while. As Leslie's pregnancy progressed, her desire to move increased also. They were constantly in search of the perfect house for their family. It was on a Tuesday evening when the house they were visiting took Leslie's breath away. As soon as she saw the house, she fell in love with it. Her feeling only grew as the Realtor led them throughout the house. She didn't even attempt to sneak off for a quick romp in one of the empty rooms. Keith saw that look in her eyes and knew this was the house for them. He admitted to himself that he found the house to be inviting. The basement would make a great man cave for him. She punched him in the arm playfully when he mentioned it to her. It was a four bedroom house with two and a half baths. The yard was huge with a circular driveway. The kitchen was by far Leslie's favorite room in the whole house. She loved the way the windows allowed the sunlight to filter in, giving it a bright and airy feel and she'd always wanted a kitchen with an adequate island. This house provided that and so much more. Plus, it looked out over a spacious backyard. They even had flowerbeds attached to each window which was a great place for her to plant some herbs.

She couldn't wait to start on a garden full of vegetables for her family. Maybe it would eventually be something they all did together as a family. She planned on exploring it further with Keith once they were settled in their new place.

The price wasn't as steep as she assumed it would be, the location was ideal, and the neighborhood was great. Keith signed the papers. Leslie jumped up and down once they finally closed. They had their new home. Things were working out wonderfully for them. Keith realized that this was what he'd been waiting on his entire life. All of his hard work and dedication to his job; the not being a playa, all of it was designing him to be with his beautiful woman. The look on her face the day they moved in had him wanting to shed a few tears right along with her.

His Leslie was overjoyed. Even though he insisted she take it slow being that she was pregnant; she still managed to get their new home together in a matter of days with the help of her friends. Instead of relaxing after work, she got busy with the decorating. Bre and Darcy were conned into helping her out with bottles of wine for them and apple juice for Leslie.

Everything eventually came together just right. Leslie's eclectic taste was throughout the house. Once she was finished, each room had a different color theme to it. She'd really wanted to paint their bedroom a lavender color, but Keith drew the line there. Instead they finally agreed on a green/brown decor for their bedroom.

They quickly fell into a routine with them becoming homebodies more and more. Their friends were always attempting to get them to hang out, but much to their dismay, they preferred being in the comforts of their own home. With that being said, they did have them over often for dinner and cards.

Keith loved the way things were going between him and Leslie. Each and every day he was excited to come home to her. They took turns with dinner and kitchen duties up until Leslie went on leave from her job in customer service. He had been trying to get her to take it much earlier but she refused saying that she had to do something. He knew she was nervous about the baby just as he was. Both nervous and super excited. He couldn't wait until he held his child in his arms for the first time.

He often sat out on the patio imagining how their baby would look. Would it have hair like Leslie? Eyes like his? If it's a boy or a girl? Leslie would laugh at him and inform him that he was being ridiculous but then he'd catch her staring off into space and knew she was thinking the same things. His Leslie was everything he'd ever wanted in a wife. She was the most beautiful woman in the world to him. She was loving and caring. Her dedication to her family and her faith was astounding. She didn't try to force her views on others. She accepted everyone's opinion as just that. Her demeanor was always happy and loving and he planned on keeping her that way. She was his to love and protect till death did them part and he vowed to spend the rest of his life doing just that.

Chapter 14

August 2010

Leslie was home by herself when she went into labor. It was around noon and Keith was still at work making his ends. She was in the middle of doing the dishes when she felt a sharp pain in her abdomen and in her lower back. With all of the women in her family telling stories about each one of their children's birth, she more than knew what to expect with her own. She went to the bedroom to try and relax and time the contractions. After about an hour the pain became unbearable for her and she called Keith to tell him it was time. He made it home in record time to escort her to the hospital.

"I'm right here with you, love." Keith whispered to Leslie as another contraction stole through her body.

"Oh God, "she cried out while squeezing his hand. "It hurts so bad."

"I know, baby. It will all be over soon." He ran his fingers through her hair trying to help relieve some of the tension in her body. Once the doctor was in position, he instructed her to push. And push is exactly what she did. With Keith standing next to the bed coaching her, Leslie gave birth to their son.

Mason Lawson was 8lbs and 2oz, looking like a miniature Keith. Tears of joy and amazement ran down his face as he cut the umbilical cord.

"Leslie baby, he's so gorgeous. Thank you so much for him. I love you." He leaned in to place a kiss upon her forehead as she held their son for the first time. He wiped the tears from her eyes and put his head to hers.

"You make me so very happy."

A smile graced her face, "Keith, look at his eyes. They are so cute." She exclaimed as she inspected her baby boy from head to toe making sure everything was accounted for.

"He's perfect, just like his mother." Keith admitted to her.

The bonding time flew by and soon the nurse was there to take the baby to the nursery so that Leslie could get some proper rest. She smiled upon entering the room. Keith had joined Leslie and Mason on the bed.

"I'm sorry to interrupt, but it's time for our new mother to get some rest. Plus, we need to run a few tests on the baby." She informed Keith as she began to wheel the bed towards the door. She looked back over her shoulder and said to him, "You can come down the hall and visit him if you wish."

"Okay, thanks." He replied. He would go and look in on his son in a little while after he made sure Leslie was good and on her way to sleep. He was still in disbelief that their son was actually there. It was all real. They were a family, his family. He held his love close as she drifted off. He stroked her hair and the side of her face until he was sure she was in a deep sleep. He placed a light kiss on her forehead then made his way to the nursery to look in on his son. Before making it to his destination, he ran into their friends exiting the elevator. A huge smile graced his face as he announced he had a son. He led them to the nursery and pointed out his son. The pride in his eyes was evident for all to see.

"He's so beautiful," Bre cried out, standing there gazing down at the baby.

"I know," Keith admitted.
"Proud papa in da house," his friend Telvin said while slapping him on the back.

"And you know it," Keith still was in amazement that he was an actual father to a real baby. He, now, had a son to teach the ways of the world and to love, hold, and cherish just as much as his Leslie.

Having a newborn in the house was a huge change for the two. They tried not to spoil their son but one of them managed to always be holding him. They took turns with the middle of the night feeding. Keith was a wonderful dad. He allowed Leslie to rest and heal from pushing out his seed. He even helped her with chores. Her parents came by from time to time to help out, but Leslie usually ended up sending them on their way once she became fed up with all of their unsolicited advice. Keith even made it a point to watch Mason one day a week to give Leslie some time to have a night out with her friends. Sometimes they went to dinner or out to a movie, just something to give her a break from being in the house all day.

Chapter 15

Keith knew damn well he should have stayed home. Even though Leslie said that she was cool with him hanging with his friends. He knew there were going to be strippers floating around. Hell, he felt confident enough in his relationship to chance it and now it was backfiring on his ass. He realized the mistake once his dick got hard for the first of many times that night. He hadn't made love to his lady in over a month and his nerves were shot.

After having a few drinks, the strippers entered and his good night turned into a very bad memory. While buzzing with a rock-hard dick, Ashlyn was able to worm her way in his pants. He needed a nut and she was available. But as soon as it was over, the regret poured in. He knew that he had messed up his good thing. He had just cheated on his fiancé whom was at home caring for their newborn baby, which was also the reason he wasn't having sex. She was still healing from pushing out his son. And here he was fucking with some bitch in a back room because he was horny. He shook his head and began getting dressed as quickly as he could.

"Where are you going?" Ashlyn asked him.

"I'm going home," he replied. His mind was in a messed up place and he needed to leave as quick as possible.

"Why, I mean we only just begun. We have all night and you didn't make me cum yet." She threw the covers back and attempted a sexy pose. That only pissed Keith off even more. He couldn't stomach the sight of her.

"Naw, I'm good. I need to go home to my family."

"Your family? Dude, you weren't thinking about your family when I was sucking your dick. You weren't thinking about them when you were nutting down my throat." She was getting pissed at the thought of him leaving her unsatisfied. Especially when she knew that he would not be getting any at home.

"You are right, I wasn't thinking about them then, but I am now. So, I'm out. I'm sorry about all of this but I have to go home." He started walking towards the door as she picked up a shoe and threw it at him.

"You make me sick you sorry excuse for a man. I freaking hate you!" She cried as he continued to the door. "Fuck you, you weak ass bitch!" she screamed at his retreating form.

He looked back at her with sad eyes before exiting the room. He knew that his home would never be the same again because as sure as he was of his name, he knew that this was going to get back to Leslie. Keith knew that it was only a matter of time before the shit hit the fan. He figured it would be best if it came from him instead of someone else. He just needed to confess and hope for the best. He would be willing to do whatever it would take to keep his relationship. Leslie was his life. All during the drive, he mentally beat himself up for falling into Ashlyn's trap. He still couldn't believe that he'd avoided her all of these years as a single man only to get caught up in her web when he was on his way to the alter. He never desired her that way. That was the messed up part. He never felt any sexual chemistry towards her in all of that time, but in one fucked up night she'd managed to worm her way inside of his pants. He shook his head in disgust as he recalled the way he allowed her to suck his dick.

He made it home in record time. He sat in his car for a moment trying to gather his thoughts. He knew he needed to go inside, but he dreaded seeing her face. Luck was on his side. Leslie was curled up in bed with their son, fast asleep. He released the breath that he was holding and took a long hot shower. He would give anything to erase the last few hours of his life. He couldn't even begin to understand what possessed him to play with his future like that. His family was his world and he knew he would lose them if she found out about what happened at that party. Before climbing into bed, he prayed harder than he ever had. He hoped God forgave cheaters too.

In the days that came, Keith's nerves were shot to hell. He knew it was only a matter of time before his secret was revealed. Ashlyn was messy and he was sure she'd be starting some shit soon. If only he was brave enough just to get it out the way and promise not to ever do some stupid crap like that again. Instead he held on to the truth, knowing that once Leslie found out, she was going to be pissed. Hell, he figured she'd probably try to leave him. He shook his head at the idea of being without his family and his heart began to ache. He knew he had to think of some way of breaking it to her before the shit really hit the fan and he lost all that he'd work so hard for. Looking Leslie in the eyes was more difficult than he imagined. It was like she could see deep down in his soul. His guilt was eating away at him on a daily basis. Keith knew the best plan of action was to admit what he did before she found out by way of gossip. He just didn't have the courage to get it over with just yet. He wasn't ready to lose his love and he knew that it was a definite possibility that she was going to leave him. She was not the kind of woman that tolerated infidelity in her relationships. His heart hurt when he thought about the possibility of not having her in his life to love and to hold each and every day. His son was his pride and joy. Would she take his son from him? Or would she allow him to at least spend some time the baby even if they ended up being apart.

"**D**ude, what the hell is up with you? You are playing like crap today. This is the damn third game we've lost in a row." Sam yelled at Keith as they took a break from their weekly game of basketball.

"My bad, man. I've been a little preoccupied lately." He told his friend as he wiped sweat from his face. He knew his mind wasn't completely into the game. He would have been better off staying home and letting them have the game to themselves instead of bringing the team down.

"You want to talk?" Sam asked him. He could see that something was going on with his friend. As far as he knew, Keith and Leslie were happy and plus they just had their baby boy. He'd always assumed they were good, better than good actually.

"Man, I messed up bad!" He admitted to him.

"Explain,"

"Fucking Ashlyn caught me slipping with her conniving ass," was all he needed to say to his friend.

"Awww, no way man. Please tell me you didn't sleep with that trick. Please tell me you have more sense than to get involved with that troubled ass woman." He looked at Keith in pure disbelief.

"She caught me, but I didn't fuck her. She gave me head and I came to my right state of mind then I burnt out before I made it worse. If Leslie finds out she's going to flip and probably leave my ass. Y'all know she doesn't play like that. You remember how it was when she was dating that jerk Stanley."

"Yeah and now your ass is the jerk. How the hell could you mess up what you guys have over some worn out, used, tired ass pussy? You know Leslie loves your ass more than anything in this world. How could you throw it all away for a damn nut that I'm sure you would have gotten at home?" Keith wasn't expecting his friend to be this upset. Sam had fire in his eyes as he ranted on and on. "Man, you have what we all want and you up and throw it away over someone that's not even worth the hassle. You know she's not going to let this shit go. You know for a fact that she's going to make sure Leslie finds out. I can't believe you, dude!"

"I know, I fucked up, but I could really use a damn friend right now instead of getting the third degree from you. What happened to having my back?" He still couldn't believe the way his boy was taking the news. If he was reacting like this, he dared imagine the way Leslie would behave. Damn, how he was going to get out of this mess, he thought to himself. He took a quick shower before heading home to his family. He felt that his time with them was limited and he needed to put in as much time as he could before the shit hit the fan and blew up in his face.

Chapter 16

October 2010

Darcy and Bre went to brunch at a mutual friend's house on a lovely Saturday. It had been raining for the past week almost. They were more than thrilled to see the sun actually shining for once. They attempted to get Leslie to join them. She was having no parts of it. Her excuse was that it was too soon to leave little Mason with someone other than his parents and since Keith was playing ball with his friends; she'd have to decline and stay home. The ladies both joked that she was making excuses because she really didn't want to part with her son. All in all, it was the truth; Leslie preferred staying home to hanging out with her friends nowadays. She liked catering to the men in her life on a daily basis. Maybe one day she'd venture out back into the world, but not anytime soon.

Darcy snatched a flute of champagne from a passing tray before scanning the room to see who all was in attendance.

She was thoroughly surprised to spot Ashlyn in the room. Her attitude made it hard for her to have any lasting friendships amongst the ladies. She wondered how she came to be at the brunch.

"Hey Bre, look who's here," she leaned over to whisper to her friend.

Bre looked around the room, not spotting her at first. "Who," she asked.

"Your girl, Ashlyn," Darcy informed her taking pity on the woman for being lost.

"What the hell is she doing here? Ugh, she makes me so damn sick that I can't even stand to be in the same room with her for long." She shook her head in disgust. A frown grew on her face and Darcy was shocked to say the least. She'd never really seen her friend have that reaction to anyone in their circle.

"What happened between the two of you? I thought you guys were thick as thieves." Darcy recalled Bre bringing Ashlyn with her on a number of outings. She'd been wondering why the woman had been missing in action for the past few months, but she didn't think much of it though.

"She's trifling and you know it. We were at a party and this guy was coming on to me. I admit it, I was really feeling him something serious. He and his friends had joined us at our table because the place was packed. I had to go to the bathroom and when I got back to the table, she was on the dance floor making out with my dude! I mean she knew I was interested but did that matter to her?

Nope, not at all. They left me at the table with his friends looking like a fucking idiot. After having two more drinks, they returned to the table and the dude had the nerves to try and pick up where we left off. He told me he wasn't interested in her and that it was just a dance, but the fact still remained that she was all over him." Bre shook her head in remembrance of her friend's deceitful ways. Darcy saw the hurt flash in her eyes momentarily before being replaced with something else.

"Dang, that's totally messed up." She admitted. That news didn't surprise her in the least bit. They all knew Ashlyn was shiesty. She was just glad that Bre found out about her before she really did some drastic crap like fuck her man or some stupid shit like that. Her mother always told her that you can't trust a hoe and Ashlyn was a straight up, gold digging, trifling, lying ass, hoe.

"Sure it, but I should have been expecting her to do me like that. Hell, she does it to everyone else why should I be any different. Friendship holds no value in her eyes. It's all about her and what she wants. That's all that matters in her world."

"She's going to eventually get hers, just you watch and see." Darcy promised her. She was a firm believer in karma and Ashlyn's ass was a prime candidate for it.

Darcy was on her way to the kitchen to escape the cackling of the ladies for a moment when she heard some voices before she entered.

"Girl, he is definitely packing, I promise you that."

"You have got to be shitting me!"

Darcy recognized the first voice as Ashlyn's. She wasn't quite sure who the other belonged to. She stood there holding her breath, wondering who and what they were talking about.

"Nope, girl, I had him nutting in less than ten minutes, toes popping and everything." Ashlyn bragged on.

"How did you manage that? I thought he was engaged to Leslie?"

"Hmph," he might be engaged, but his dick told me otherwise that night. And I guarantee I'm going to be getting some more of that sometime soon." She made it clear that something was going on with them. Darcy couldn't believe her ears. Keith was messing around on Leslie after she'd just given birth to his son. This had to be the most lowdown dirty shit that he'd ever done. She slowly closed the door and ran to find Bre to let her know what she'd found out. After making up a reason for them to leave early, she practically dragged her friend to the car and pushed her inside.

"Damn Darcy, what in the hell is all of that about?" Bre demanded.

"Girl you would never believe what I just heard,"

"What, spill it," she pleaded with her.

"I just heard Ashlyn telling someone that she has been fucking Keith. She was going into details about how his damn dick looks and all." Darcy let the words flow from her mouth without taking a breather.

"No fucking way! He can't be that damn stupid. I mean, after the way he pursued Leslie, he cheated? No, I can't believe that shit." Bre said.

"I know my cuz and I know Ashlyn is not even his type in the least bit. He could never stand her bitchy ass attitude at all. Man, this is some messed up stuff for real." Her mind began wondering if it was her place to alert her girlfriend on what was happening or keep her cousin's secret until the shit was exposed. And she knew that eventually it was going to

96

be all out in the streets. She felt a stab of sympathy for Leslie. She'd allowed herself to fall in love with Keith. She believed in their happily ever after. Now, here she was, trying to determine if it would be best to shatter her friend's dreams or just be there for her once it happened on its own.

Chapter 17

"Why are you acting like this, girl?" Leslie asked her girlfriend. Darcy had been avoiding her calls and when she did finally corner her into having lunch with her. Her friend was hardly even talking to her. She knew something was up. She raked her brain trying to remember if she had forgotten some important date or if she had unintentionally done something to offend her.

"Nothing, work has been having me stressed out, that's all." Her friend told her. Leslie read her face and knew she wasn't being honest with her.

"Look, we have known one another for a long time. We've been through all kinds of shit together. If I have done something to piss you off, I wish you would let me know so I can at least try and fix it." She told Darcy, hoping to appeal to her sensitive side...Darcy took a deep breath and looked Leslie in the eyes. She then lowered her head while fiddling with her hands. Leslie grabbed her hands.

"Darcy, what is it?" The panic flashed in Leslie's light brown eyes.

"Leslie, you know I love you right?" Darcy glanced around the café before continuing the dreaded conversation. She'd come to the conclusion that Leslie needed to know what was going on with her future husband, even if it was her own flesh and blood. Wrong was wrong and she felt he was dead wrong doing his family the way he supposedly did. "I've been hearing a rumor. At first, I assumed it was a rumor, but now I know otherwise."

"Okay, what rumor? Girl, you know I haven't been in the mix for a while. This is the first time I've really been out since having the baby. You have got to catch me up on all of the things I've missed." Leslie got comfortable in her seat ready to let her friend bring her up to speed.

"Um…there was this thing going around about Keith." Darcy was fiddling with the straw in her drink. Leslie wanted to grab her hand and demand that she tell her what the hell she was talking about. She knew patience was a virtue, but her patience was running thin with her friend at the moment.

"What about Keith?" The look on Darcy's face let Leslie know that she was not about to be thrilled with what she had to say. "Come on, Darcy, tell me what the hell has been going on." She urged her friend to continue.

Darcy took a deep breath before continuing, "Okay here it is…there was a rumor going around that Keith cheated on you."

Leslie let what she said sink in. It felt like her heart was about to thump on out of her chest. "With who?" She managed to finally ask. She had her suspicions, but she wanted to wait and find out first. Darcy didn't say anything for a long moment.

"Who did he fuck, Darcy?" Leslie's voice was laced with anger. Her friend jumped in her seat when she heard the question.

"Ashlyn," she whispered. Leslie sat there taking it all in, the way people were looking at her; the way Keith had been acting all guilty. She assumed it was because she was stuck at home with a newborn while he was still able to be out and about, going to work and interacting with other adults.

Now, she realized that look was because he was out fucking some other bitch while she was home caring for his son, the son that he claimed to love more than anything else in the world. The more she thought on it, the more her anger rose. She stood up from the table, "Thanks for lunch," as she was about to walk off, Darcy reached out and grabbed her arm.

"Leslie, I don't know if the shit is true or not. I just couldn't stand the fact of being around you without letting you know about it. Talk to him about it before doing anything drastic." She was trying to reason with her friend but Leslie was beyond that point.

"I'm good, girl. I know it's true. I don't have to trying and find out if it is. His actions are proof of it. Thanks for telling me, but I got this. I'll call you later." She rushed out of the café before Darcy could intercept her again.

The drive home seemed to take forever when all she wanted was to be at home with her lovelies laying in bed and watching television. That wouldn't be happening on this day.

Depending on what Keith admitted to would determine if they were over or not. She vowed to never let a man use her in any kind of way. Cheating was a no-no to her way of thinking. There was no way she would be able to forgive him. She made her way into the house. The delicious smells hit her first before she heard the jazz on the stereo. Then she heard the clink of some dishes. She followed the sounds into the kitchen. He was standing at the stove cooking dinner. His jeans hung low on his hips and his t-shirt was hugging him just like she liked it. The site broke her heart knowing that this could be the end of them. He turned and noticed her standing there.

"Hey baby, when did you get home?" He walked over to her and placed a kiss on her lips. He pulled her close and nuzzled her cheek before placing a kiss in the same spot.

"Just now," she replied, trying to keep her emotions in check.

"How was it? Did you girls have fun shopping and gossiping?" He pulled her further into his body and put his nose to her neck and inhaled deeply.

"Um...it was interesting to say the least." She thought back to her conversation with Darcy.

"Oh yeah?" he let his kisses linger on her skin.

"Sure was…how was your day?" She asked as she slid her arms around his neck. She needed him to hold her tight before she asked him.

"I've been missing you, love. You know I don't like to be away from you for too long." His lips captured hers swallowing her next reply. She gave in to him and let him control their kiss. Once he released her lips he looked deep in her eyes and said, "I love you so much, Leslie. You make me so damn happy, baby." Upon hearing those words, she let loose on him. She tried to contain her fury to give him time to admit to it, but she couldn't any longer.

"Did you fuck Ashlyn?" Her voice was low as she asked the question, getting right to the point.

"What...what are you talking about?" His gazed faltered just enough for her to catch it. He looked terrified and fucking guilty as hell.

"I'm talking about the fact that people are saying you fucked her while I was home with your son. That's what I'm talking about!" His arms fell to his side as his look changed from terrified to sorrow. Her heart broke into a million pieces at that exact moment. "You did it, didn't you?"

"Leslie, baby, let me explain..." he started saying. Leslie turned and walked out of the kitchen without allowing him to finish what he was saying. She didn't hear his footsteps following her and for that she was grateful. She wasn't up for dealing with him at the moment. She ran up the stairs and entered their bedroom. She looked around their room thinking of the day they decorated it. Her eyes fell upon the king size bed in the middle of the room. She wondered if he had fucked someone else on it. The thought of that had her dropping to her knees as sobs raked her body. Strong arms wrapped around her body as her cries faded.

"I'm so sorry, Leslie. I never meant to hurt you." His eyes pleaded with her, begging her to forgive him for his transgressions.

"It's too late for that," she screamed as she pushed him away. She scrambled to her feet. There was only one thing left to do. She made her way to the closet and pulled out her suitcase.

102

"What are you doing?" Keith's voice was laced with panic.

"What does it look like? I'm leaving," she told him as she grabbed items from the closet. As soon as she placed something in the suitcase, Keith removed it.

"No, you aren't going anywhere. Baby, let's talk about this. I didn't sleep with her, I promise."

"Oh no, then why the guilty look, why are you apologizing if nothing happened?"

"I stopped myself before it got that far," he admitted to her.

"How far did it get, Keith?" She knew she really didn't want to hear the details. She needed to know.

"Leslie," his eyes begged her not to make him go any further. She stood rooted in that spot while looking at the man she thought she would be spending the rest of her life with. She closed her eyes and took a deep breath before speaking, "We're leaving."

"I can't let you do that." He continued removing items from her bag as she placed them in.

"Keith, stop," she cried, pushing him away from her suitcase.

"No, you aren't leaving me! I fucking love you!" She'd never seen him look like this before. He was determined not to let her leave. His eyes were red and she could see veins popping out in his neck. She cleared her head and erased the sympathy. The matter at hand was that he'd cheated on her with a woman he knew she didn't like. He'd basically handed the bitch ammunition.

"If you loved me then you shouldn't have been with that bitch. Now, leave me alone."

"No, you aren't taking my son and you are not leaving this fucking house. Do I make myself clear?" The boom of his voice startled Leslie. Fear took over the anger and hurt. She backed up against the wall and watched as he put her clothes back up and put the suitcase away. He grabbed her purse, took her keys, and placed them in his pocket. He even went as far as to take her money and credit cards out of her wallet and her cell phone. "I can't lose you, Leslie. I'm in love with you. I know I messed up but baby I can't let you leave me like this. I need you in my life. Please give me a chance to make this better. We can get through this if you just give us the time to do it instead of attempting to run away." He walked over to her and placed a kiss on her forehead before leaving the room to lock her things up in his safe.

Leslie didn't know what to do. She was cut off from everyone at the moment. The last thing she wanted to do was remain with him, but that was her only option at the moment. So she sat on the bed thinking of a way to leave without his knowledge. She knew she had to have plan, if not, it would all be for naught.

She played along with him for the rest of the night. When he called her for dinner, she joined him. He attempted to draw her into the conversation to no avail. He wouldn't let her leave, but he couldn't make her talk to him. She said not one word to him for the rest of the night. She interacted with their son, but refused to utter one single word to him. With her silence, he tried to explain as best he could about that night. Even with his honesty, she knew that she couldn't remain with him. If it was that easy for him to be tempted, then she didn't need to be with him.

Cheating was a big no-no in her eyes. The one thing she detested the most, right along with abuse. He hadn't reached that point yet, but she wasn't going to take any chances. If someone would have asked her yesterday if she thought Keith was capable of abuse, she would have laughed and said definitely not, but on this day, she was not sure of anything any longer. All she knew was that she had to leave before things got worse for either of them. She refused to raise her son in a broken home. The remainder of the weekend was torture for them both, with Keith trying his best to work things out. Trying to prove to her that it was a horrible mistake and with her is where he wanted to be. Leslie held on to her silence, only interacting with the baby. She had even stopped sharing meals with him. It broke his heart to see her shut herself off from him like that, but he didn't know what to do to make it better. He had no idea how to eradicate the situation. His future with Leslie would forever be changed.

On Monday, he wanted to stay home. He needed to stay home, but life wouldn't allow it. He had been off for a few weeks with Leslie after the birth of their son. So, he had to put in some time at work. Keith still hadn't given her things back because he feared that if he did, she was sure to leave him. He felt that if she didn't have the means, then she would have no choice but to remain at home. He knew for a fact that she hated borrowing anything from anyone at any time. So, he held on to the hope that she wouldn't do it.

The work day seemed to drag on for him. He made mistake after mistake throughout the morning. Lunch hour finally rolled around and he picked up his phone to call her. The phone went straight to voicemail. He was about to dial her number again before he realized that he had her phone locked up in his safe. He shook his head and took a deep breath. Loving Leslie was all that he wanted to do. Loving Leslie was his way of life. He didn't think he could handle losing her. He managed to clear his head for the second part of his shift. At quitting time, he raced out of the building, anxious to get home to his family. Plotting on a way to make Leslie understand and forgive him.

Chapter 18

Leslie's mind had been in overdrive all weekend. She had a plan and she knew it was foolproof. He thought he could make her stay, but in reality, it only made her that much more determined. She loved Keith with everything in her, but there was no way she could/would stay.

She wasn't sure that he'd go to work on Monday because he said as much. But when he walked out the door, she breathed a sigh of relief. Her opportunity had arisen. It was time to make her escape. She knew she had to be careful being that her best friend was his family. There was no one to turn to without them attempting to try and convince her to stay with him. She had to get away and far away at that. Leslie smirked at the thought of Keith thinking he had her trapped. She made light work of packing her and Mason's things.

Then she went to the neighbors and asked if she could use their phone. Her excuse was that she couldn't find hers and she thought that she'd left it in Keith's car. They seemed satisfied with her explanation and left her to make her call. She summoned a cab to her residence and once it arrived. She had the driver to help her load her suitcases in the back and instructed him to take her to the bank. She had an emergency account set up separate from everything else. Once inside the bank, she emptied her account and headed to the airport.

Leslie bought a plane ticket for the first flight out which happened to be going to Columbia, South Carolina. She didn't know anyone there, but she didn't care. She needed to be alone without people trying to give her unsolicited advice and she couldn't do that back home. She needed her space. Once the plane landed, she exhaled. She hadn't realized that she was holding her breath the whole time. Thankfully Mason had slept majority of the flight.

It gave her time to think of how she would proceed. She worked her budget and determined the best plan of action for her to take. She asked around for a decent, inexpensive hotel when one of the agents informed her that his apartment complex had openings and they were a fare price, depending on how long she was in town for.

He assured her that she would come out better getting the apartment especially since they had a move-in special going. She was leery at first until one of his co-workers; a tall white woman with long auburn hair joined the conversation. She confirmed everything the guy had told her being that she lived there also. She informed her that the area was decent and the manager was good about working with people. They gave her the number and address to the place. It was her second stop after securing a room and putting up their things. Before heading over to the complex, she called the manager and asked all of the particulars. It all seemed doable. She had enough money for at least five months of rent. She planned on applying for work once she found a decent daycare for her son. It would be the first time, but she had to do what was necessary to survive.

On the drive home, Keith felt a wave of uneasiness wash through his body. Something wasn't right. His foot pressed down on the gas pedal as he sped through town trying to get home in record time. He had barely shut his engine before he jumped out of the car and ran to the door. The house had an eerie silence. Not a sound was heard at all. His heart hammered in his chest. His mind was refusing to believe what his eyes and heart told him. After all of the precautions he took to keep her there, she still managed to leave and take his son with her. The house suddenly felt completely empty. He dropped to his knees as sobs raked through his body.

His family was gone and it wasn't a damn thing he could do about it. Once his cries subsided, he took survey of the place. Her car was still there. He still had her phone and her money. Someone had to know something and he was determined to find out what. He called their friends and none of them knew a thing. Nobody had heard from her since Friday. He was up against a brick wall. He had no way of finding out anything. He slump on the couch as defeat entered his bones. The inevitable had happened. He'd lost his Leslie and she'd taken his son with her. His family was gone and he had no earthy idea as to where they would go. His chest constricted and it was like he couldn't catch his breath. He felt like he was going to have a heart attack. He was lost. He was alone and he didn't even know which way was up.

Chapter 19

The new place was working out quite lovely for them even though she missed Keith like crazy. Her apartment was a small one bedroom with very affordable rent. She found work at a bookstore/coffee shop not too far from where she lived. She was able to walk to and from work. For that she was thankful because she really didn't want to spend any extra money on a car when she didn't need it. The community she lived in was a close one. People there took the time out to get to know one another. They made it a point to speak when they saw you out. At first it was a bit much, but after a few weeks, they had claimed her as one of their own. She even found a babysitter that resided in the same complex. She was an older lady that lived off of social security and watched children from time to time. All of the kids in the area loved her dearly which made the decision for Leslie much easier than she'd originally thought.

Life was simple, painful, but very simple. She called her parents and her friends to let them know she and Mason were okay. They tried their best to get her to spill her location. She always ended the call once their questions started heading in the wrong direction. She missed Keith horribly. Even though he cheated, she still craved his touch. She missed him holding her in his arms as they lay in bed. She missed the feeling of protection.

Dating had no room in her life, so when one of the tenants in the next complex asked her out, she refused the invitation without even considering it. She explained to him that she was going through a very painful breakup and she didn't think it would be fair of her to lead him on when she knew for a fact that her heart would not be involved in it. The guy understood and thanked her for being honest with him. That didn't stop him from speaking to her each and every day. She had recently begun looking forward to his smile in the mornings. The way his eyes lit up when he smiled was often brighter than the sun and it always managed to lift Leslie's spirits no matter how rough her day was going which she'd forever be grateful for because she didn't have much to be happy about besides her son growing beautifully.

Keith was living in a state of total disbelief. His love had actually left him and took his son with her. He didn't actually think she would up and leave him like this, leave the fucking state with no contact. He had no way of finding them. He was an emotional wreck by the end of the first week without his family. His thoughts often strayed to harming Ashlyn for her role in all that had transpired. Weeks came and went without a word from her.

Everyone now knew that she had taken their son and left him high and dry. She did call her mother and Darcy just to let them know that she was okay, but she didn't reveal her location. Darcy told Keith that Leslie confessed that she was no longer in the same state as them. She said she needed time to heal and she couldn't do that with everyone in her business. She told him that Mason was doing great and Leslie had promised to send pictures eventually.

The conversation did little to ease his hurt. Darcy hated seeing him so broken but there wasn't a thing she could do to help him. He'd brought this all on himself and in the process lost the two people that meant the most to him in this world. Leslie was her best friend and he'd managed to take that away from her too. She wanted to slap him for allowing Ashlyn to break up his home. She wasn't worth it at all. She was a whore and a home wrecker. Everyone knew what she was about and her stupid ass cousin got caught slipping.

"Darcy, can you convince her to come home?" Keith slurred. He had been drinking nonstop for the past week. His house was a complete mess. There were empty beer cans and liquor bottles everywhere. He smelled horrible and he was in need of a haircut.

"She doesn't want to talk about it. When I try and bring it up, she ends the call." She told him. "Would you really want her to come back and see you like this?" She shook her head. She loved her cousin and she hated to see him like this. He was a shell, no longer vibrant and full of life. He no longer cared about his looks. He didn't care about anything at all anymore. They were all worried sick about his mental state.

"If I can't have my family back then I don't give a fuck. Fuck all of this shit, it means nothing to me without them, cuz." Tears welled up in his eyes. He got up and stumbled to the kitchen to grab another beer.

"Have you eaten today?" she asked him. She could tell that he'd lost some weight. He was in a downward spiral, hell-bent on self-destruction.

"Fuck food," he said before downing his beer in one big gulp. He threw the can on the floor and grabbed another one.

"Why are you doing this? Come on, Keith this is not the way." Darcy pleaded with him, trying to make him see reasoning. He shrugged his shoulders and went to lie on the couch. She didn't know what else to do or to say. Instead, she did what she could and starting cleaning up the house. She went grocery shopping and put the food away. At least there would be something in the fridge for him to eat when the urge hit him.

That night she prayed that Keith would wake up and realize what he was doing to himself and how he was making everyone worry about him. They were all afraid he was going to end up hurting himself rather it was intentional or not. All she could do was try and be there for him to the best of her abilities without passing judgment and making him slip further into depression.

She could see how much this situation was affecting him. At first, she was pissed at what he did to Leslie, but when she found out the real truth, Keith had her sympathy. He got caught slipping for real. True enough, his ass shouldn't have been in that position to begin with.

He should have been home loving on his baby boy instead. But she couldn't fault him for wanting to hang out after being in the house for an extended period of time. Everybody needed a break every now and again, it's what you choose to do while on said break that matters. True, he was her family, but she was a woman first. Cheating is cheating and Leslie had her sympathy in more ways than one. She prayed they'd be able to repair their broken relationship and become the family God intended for them to be.

Chapter 20

Leslie was reaching beneath the counter at the bookstore where she worked, to pick up a pen that fell when she heard the bell above the door chime. In walked a guy accompanied by a toddler. They made their way over to the children's section. She went back to doing her paperwork while they browsed. After a while, she made her way over to them and asked if they needed help with anything. He turned to her and stared for a minute. She began to feel intimidated at the way he was looking at her. Her hand slowly crept up to her face attempting to feel and see if she had anything on her face.

"Excuse me for staring, but your eyes are extremely beautiful." He said to her when he was finally able to speak.

"Um, thank you," she stammered. He continued to take her in from head to toe without being shy in the least bit.

"I haven't seen you here before. Are you new to the area?" He asked her.

"Yes, I've been here about a month." She admitted to him, wondering if he was one of the regulars that she was told about by the manager of the store.

"Hmm, I think I need to have a word with my cousin about keeping secrets from me."

"Your cousin?" Leslie was lost with the conversation and the direction it was headed in.

"Yes, she owns the store. Usually she consults with me before hiring someone new. I guess it slipped her mind this time." He shook his head in disbelief. Leslie felt herself calming down tremendously once it was known that he was a part of her manager's family instead of a complete stranger trying to hit on her.

"So, who do we have here?" Leslie asked him as she squatted down to the kid's level and smiled at the little girl. She was simply adorable with her big brown chocolate eyes and full lips.

"This is my baby girl, Blossom. Sweetie, say hi to the nice lady." He encouraged his daughter. The beautiful little girl glanced up at Leslie from behind her father's leg. She didn't look like she had any intention of speaking so Leslie took the lead.

"Aren't you just gorgeous? I bet your daddy is proud to have a baby girl like you." She smiled at Blossom.

"I sure am, baby." Her dad added to the conversation between the two of them.

"My daddy says that I'm his little princess," she finally came from around his legs and said to Leslie.

"I'm sure you are. I know that my baby is my little prince." She knew how little girls generally felt about babies.

Just as she expected, Blossom was intrigued by the mere mention of Mason.

"Ooh, you have a baby? Is it a girl or a boy?" Her bright inquisitive eyes held Leslie's as she awaited the answers to her questions.

Leslie smiled before answering, "Yes, I have a baby boy and his name is Mason. He is the light of my life and he isn't even walking yet so he's a really little baby."

"I love little babies," the little girl exclaimed happily, "I keep asking my daddy to give me one, but he says that I need a mother first. My mommy went to heaven to be with my granny. I miss her so much." Sadness washed over Leslie as she glanced up at the man. She could see the hurt still there in his eyes. Her heart went out to them at that very moment.

"I'm so very sorry to hear that. I'm sure your dad will give you a brother or sister as soon as the time is right." She really didn't know what to say after an admission like the one she just heard.

"Thanks," replied the man. "Oh, by the way, excuse my manners. My name is Derek." He held out his hand waiting for Leslie to return the gesture.

"I'm Leslie as I'm sure you know by now." She smiled at him.

"Leslie, hmm, a nice name for a beautiful lady I would love to get to know more about. How does dinner tomorrow night at my place sound to you?" His eyes twinkled in the store light.

"I don't know, I mean we just met and you want me to come to your house? I don't think that would be a good ideal." She was unsure on how to proceed with turning him down even though her interest was peaked slightly.

LOVING LESLIE

"By the two of us having dinner at my place, neither one of us would be pressed to find a babysitter at the last minute. I don't know about you but sometimes it's hard to come up on one at times." He told her. She smiled inwardly because she knew for a fact what he said was the absolute truth. Finding a babysitter was worse than looking for a job at times.

"So, it will be just us and our babies?" she asked him while stealing a look at his daughter to see how she felt about her father asking a woman out in front of her. She didn't seem as if she mind at all in fact she looked excited.

"Will you please bring your baby so I can play with him?" She pleaded with Leslie and there was no way she could resist those oh so gorgeous eyes bearing down in her soul.

"Yes, please have dinner with us and bring your baby so we can all meet and have a wonderful time. No pressure or anything. Just two single parents getting together for a dinner play date amongst our children." He winked at her.

"That would be wonderful except the fact that my kid won't really be up running around playing with Blossom."

"True, but who's to say that he won't enjoy himself watching her running around and performing for him." His logic did make a ton of sense to her. She found herself wanting to spend time with them away from the store. Plus, she had no one to hang out with here and she was getting lonelier by the day. She needed someone or something to divert her attention from the fact that she missed Keith so damn much at times that she almost convinced herself to go home and work things out with him and try to make things work. Her rules no longer seemed as dire as they were before everything happened.

She was surprised to find out Derek lived ten minutes from her apartment which was convenient for her since she took the bus to his place. He suggested picking them up, to his dismay, she declined. She wasn't sure if giving him her address so early would be a wise thing to do on her part. She worked up the courage to knock on the door which opened instantly.

"You made it," Derek seemed excited to see her standing there.

"I told you I would." She smiled at his expression.

"I know, but I wasn't sure if you'd back out or not. Blossom's looking forward to meeting your son." He said to her while ushering them in. She heard the squeal before she saw the girl flying around the corner.

"Hey, hey, slow down, roadrunner." Her father said to her.

"You're here, you're here. You want to see my room? Is that your baby? Can I see him? Can I hold him?" The questions flew out of her mouth without her stopping to take a breather. Leslie didn't know if she should wait for a breaking point or just let her run out of steam before answering her.

"She can only answer one question at a time." Derek reminded her as he led Leslie to the living room.

"Have a seat and I'll get you something to drink. Wine okay?"

"Sure," she answered while taking in the room. Much to her surprise, it was relatively neat for a single dad. She saw a few toys scattered here and there, but she didn't spot any dust. He even had the place decorated to give off a homey feel. African art adorn the walls and African artifacts were throughout the living room. She loved the rustic charm of the place. Blossom took a seat right next to her.

"May I see your baby now?" She asked politely.

"Sure," she removed the blanket from her son and sat him up on her lap so the little girl could get a good look at him. "His name is Mason."

"Awww, he's so adorable," she said in that cute little girly voice. Mason chose that time to reach out and grab a hold of one of her fingers which thrilled her to no end. Leslie smiled at the interaction between the two of them.

"One glass of wine coming up, I hope you like red." Derek called out from behind her. Once he noticed her hands were full, he placed her glass on the table.

"I can make them a pallet on the floor so you can have your hands free." He suggested to her.

"That would be great," she said in return. He left the room only to return quickly carrying two blankets. He spread them out and had Blossom go get some of her old toys for the baby to play with. Leslie put him down on the floor and took her seat. The conversation with him wasn't forced at all. In fact, she enjoyed herself immensely. It was close to midnight before she finally stood up to gather their things.

"I know you don't think I'm letting you guys take a bus at this time of night."

"We'll be fine. It's a quick ride, actually only one bus to get home." She informed him while still packing up Mason's things. Derek was standing in front of her in a flash, "Look Leslie, there is no way in hell I'm letting you leave here at this hour. I can make up the spare room for you guys or however you want to do it, but you are staying." His tone let her know there would be no arguing with him on the topic. She gave in and allowed him to lead her to the room opposite his. As she trailed behind him, she got a very good look at him from behind. He was simply beautiful and with an attitude to match. He would be an awesome catch for someone else, just not her. She wasn't ready to allow another man in her life just yet. Her wounds weren't quite healed. She still missed Keith in the worst way. Sometimes she still cried herself to sleep after a trying day.

"I hope the room is okay for you." Derek broke her train of thought bringing her back to the present. She looked around the room in surprise. It was well kept like everything in his home.

"It's great. All we need is a bed and cover, the rest is irrelevant." She waved her hand through the air as if it wasn't a big deal that he'd given her a room with a huge bed that looked as if it was calling her name. The room seemed to be larger than her whole apartment.

"Okay, since we've established you are staying here tonight. Do you want to put Mason in here now or let him remain on the pallet until you're ready to go to bed?" He asked her.

"Who's to say I'm not ready at the moment," she joked.

"Me," he answered. "It's been a long time since I've entertained and I must admit that I'm having a wonderful time. I'm not ready for it to end just yet. So, let's have a few more drinks, watch a couple of shows and get to know one another even better." He held out his hands and smiled at her. With him looking at her like that, she couldn't form the words to deny him of his simple request. It wasn't like he was looking for more than friendship which she was thankful for. She didn't want to have to turn him down.

"Okay, fine, you twisted my arm. Where's the liquor?" she asked as she made her way back to the living room.

"One glass of wine and a beer coming right up." He called out to her.

"Make that two beers, I'm living in the fast lane tonight." He laughed at her while grabbing another can of beer from the fridge.

"That's what I'm talking about. Relax and release all of the tension from this hectic week."

"How do you know if my week has been hectic because I sure as heck don't remember saying anything to that extreme?" Leslie's look challenged him.

"Suga, you didn't have to, it's written all over your face and body. You seem tense as hell. I was going to offer you a massage but I didn't want you getting any ideals about trying to seduce me and all." His innocence act was too much for her and the laughter flew out before she could contain it.

"You're so full of yourself right now," she shook her head.

"Hmm, I just might be. Or maybe I'm just full of all this damn beer you got me drinking." At that he took a long drink to emphasis his point.

"Oh so now I'm the negative influence?"

"Yep, you got it. You know I'm a good boy. You got me partaking in all kinds of negativity tonight. Peer pressure is a mutha." His eyes twinkled with amusement.

"Is that right?" Leslie had to admit she was really enjoying their friendly banter.

"Yep,"

"I seem to recall a certain guy forcing me to do all of the talking and most of the drinking and when I wanted to leave, he twisted my arm into staying the night at his house without assuring me that I'd be safe." The liquor was making her tongue all loosey goosey.

"I didn't assure you of your safety because I'm still not too sure about all of that myself." He simply said to her.

"What do you mean," she knew the conversation was heading in the wrong direction.

"I mean that I would love nothing more than to spend the night with you in my arms and your legs wrapped around my waist." Leslie was about to protest when he held up his hands. "Please, let me finish. Even though that's what I want, I know it's not what you need, so I'm not going to press the issue. I know you aren't ready for all of that just yet. I'm content with us only being friends."

She took a deep breath before allowing herself to speak. "I don't think I'll be ready for a relationship for a long while. I'm still very much in love with Mason's father even though we aren't together."

"I can see that and I'm not trying to rush you into anything. What I would like to know is how did he manage to let you get away from him?" He looked deep into her eyes while awaiting her answer to his question.

"Ha ha, if I knew the answer to that we'd probably still be together. All I know is that he didn't love me the way I thought he did if he was tempted to cheat so easily." She sat down, as memories of the past assaulted her. Derek knelt down in front of her and took her hands into his. She blinked back the tears that were threatening to spill.

"A man doesn't always plan to cheat. Sometimes things happen to weaken his defenses. I'm not making excuses for him, but it couldn't have been him just doing it for the sheer joy of it. It has to be more to it than that. I can't see him ever wanting to lose you and Mason."

"Well, he did," she said to him. Pulling her hands from his, she stood and began pacing the room. "I was home nursing our son. He was only a month old. We weren't being intimate because I'd just had his baby. I convinced him to go hang out with his friends instead of hovering over Mason and I like we were about to break. He didn't really want to leave us, but I stood strong. I guess it was my fault that he slipped, if he'd been at home it never would have happened and my family would still be intact."

"You can't possibly know that for sure. And it is definitely not your fault that he got caught up in the moment. The woman took advantage of his moment of weakness and things probably escalated quickly. Did he continue seeing her afterwards?" Leslie didn't know why but she felt compelled to spill it all to him. Besides, it felt good to talk about it with someone who wasn't there.

"No, they didn't have an affair. He told me that they didn't go all the way. That he came to his senses before they actually had intercourse."

"So what did happen?"

"She gave him head," Leslie felt the bile rising at the thought of Ashlyn's mouth on Keith. She visibly trembled as an image popped in her mind.

"You left him because of that?" The surprise was evident in his voice. She turned and frowned at him.

"Yes I did. If he allowed that to happened, whose to say he'd be able to stop himself the next time. I can't live my life wondering what if and if he's being faithful" She was attempting to get him to see her point of view. Her actions were validated to her. There shouldn't be any reason for proving a point to him. Besides, they'd just met one another, they weren't even friends yet.

"Obviously he cares about you. At least he did have the decency to stop things before they got out of hand. True, he never should have allowed himself to be in that position, but I know for a fact that it takes a hell of a lot of willpower to stop when you're in the heat of the moment. He didn't go all the way because of his love for you and that's saying something. From the things you've said here tonight. You two still have unfinished business to attend to and it's not going to happen if you keep running from it. You know just as well as I do that Mason needs his father in his life." His words struck something deep within her core. She knew she dealt with the situation rather harshly without giving him the chance to prove his point. In her defense, she was hurting, she'd been there before and it wasn't a place she ever wanted to visit again.

"I'm so confused. At times all I want to do is pack up and go home, but then I think of him and her together and the anger returns. I miss him so damn much." She admitted to Derek.

"I know you do. Look, sometimes we have to learn how to forgive in order to be happy. I'm not saying be a fool. We're all allowed to make mistakes. It's what we do to correct them that make us better. I would give anything to be able to hold my wife in my arms again even if only just for five damn minutes. Life is too short not to hold on to true love when you have it. Trust me, I've had it and lost it, but I'll never regret one thing about it." His eyes were sad. Her heart went out to him and Blossom. It was obvious that he'd loved his wife unconditionally. "Forgive him; give him a chance to prove his worth and for him to right his wrong."

"I don't know," she began, but he cut her off.

"Imagine not ever seeing him again. Imagine your son having to grow up without a father when you knew it was in your power to at least give them that time before he was taken away from this world. Just think if he were to die in a car accident as we speak, do you think you'd spend the rest of your days living with regret?"

His questions hit their mark. He made her think long and hard about her relationship with Keith and what it was she wanted from him. After a few minutes of silence, she looked up at him, "Thanks so much for this night and the conversation. You're right; I have to learn how to forgive him. And I have to do it sooner rather than later because tomorrow isn't promised to any of us." She conceded to him.

"Exactly," he said as he raised his can in a toast to her.

Derek turned out to be a good listening partner for her during the time she spent in South Carolina. They'd often get together and hang out letting the kids play together. Even though Mason was only a baby, Blossom loved spending time with the both of them. Leslie suspected it had something to do with her losing her mother at such a young age. Leslie didn't mind showering the girl with attention and love as much as she could while she was around.

Derek more than convinced her that it was time she made up her mind about returning home to Keith. She understood where he was coming from, she was almost ready to make that trip and reconcile with her love. Mason needed his father just as much as she needed Keith back in her life. After spending so much time with her friend, she said a prayer for him to find love all over again each and every night.

She knew he deserved happiness and she hoped he embraced it once he found it. His faith was strong even after the hand they were dealt. He was raising his baby to the best of his ability with lots of love and positive reinforcement. Anyone could tell she was his world, his strength to go on, his very own blessing in disguise. She knew she would miss them a lot when the time came for her to finally leave. Derek made her promise to keep in contact with them even if it was only to let him know how things were going with her and Keith. She knew it would be more than that. The bond they formed required more than a simple phone call. Theirs was a friendship she cherished and one she'd keep for as long as he was willing to be there.

Chapter 21

Keith was constantly in a drunken stupor. Alcohol was his new best friend. He had been at Conrad's bar since around eight and it was nearing midnight. The bartender was hesitant about giving him another drink.

"Man, why don't you have someone to come and pick you up." His attention was focused on wiping down the bar, but he kept glancing at Keith from the corner of his eyes.

"I'm good," Keith slurred. He turned and almost fell off the bar stool. He fumbled with the stool and bar trying to right himself before he toppled to the floor. The lady seated next to him took his arm and lifted him up.

"No you aren't. I can't give you another drink." He didn't want to be responsible if something happened to the young man when he could have prevented it.

"My money ain't good here?" Keith asked the bartender with an attitude.

"Just go on home and sleep it off."

"There is nothing or no one at home for me." His voice was low. The bartender noticed his eyes watering and felt a stab of sympathy for him.

"Look, how about I call you a cab so you won't have to worry about driving home?" He asked him. Regardless of the answer, he wasn't allowing the guy to leave his bar and drive as drunk as he was.

"Whatever, just as long as you bring me another drink." His attention turned to the woman sitting next to him. She was wearing one of those short fuck me dresses and sky high heels. He knew she was on a mission. His pants tightened when he noticed that her nipples were hard.

"You know I can give you a ride home if you like," The woman said to Keith. There was a look of pure lust in her eyes and he was not drunk enough to miss it.

"That sounds like a plan to me," he responded to her and placed a hand on her bare thigh. He squeezed slightly and she closed her eyes momentarily.

"Maybe we should leave right now," she threw out while licking her ruby red lips. Keith usually didn't go for dating outside of his race, but he hadn't been intimate with anyone since Leslie. He was hoping the woman could ease some of his hurt if only for the time being.

"Let's go," he stood and took her hand. He threw forty dollars on the bar and they left, hand in hand with the bartender shaking his head, hoping the young man knew what he was doing.

Keith's eyes rolled back in his head when her lips wrapped around his dick. It had been so long since he'd felt pleasure that he was sure he wouldn't be able to last for long. She picked up the pace, slurping and deep throating him.

The familiar pressure started to build and he knew it was only a matter of time before he exploded.

"Cum for me, daddy," she said around his dick.

"Oh fuck," he cried as she took him all the way in. There was no time to warn her before he squirted his load down her throat. She continued sucking him until he was back hard like she wanted him. The blood was flowing and he was ready to fuck her as hard as he could. He found the energy to flip her over and began ripping her clothes off. All the while she's begging him to slow down and let her control things.

He paid no attention to her words as he snapped her panties off. Her eyes were wide as she looked at him. Keith was frozen in his spot. His mind was trying to process what was going on. His stomach started turning violently and the anger started to build. The woman that was lying beneath him was not a woman, but a man. A man with a hard dick that was slightly bigger than his. He had breast and looked like a woman except for the dick between its legs. His mind snapped as he fastened his pants.

The he/she opened his mouth to say something. That something was held in his throat as Keith's hands tried to squeeze the life from his body. Upon releasing him, he took to pummeling the guys face repeatedly until his was exhausted. The noise had people in the neighboring rooms calling the cops. They burst through the door to see Keith stomping a naked body with blood all over the bed and his clothing.

"Freeze," one cop yelled while training his gun on Keith.

"Fuck that, Imma kill this bitch," Keith was damn near foaming at the mouth. One of the cops wrestled him to the ground and placed handcuffs on him while the he/she scrambled to put on clothing.

"Care to explain what is going on?" cop one asked the man.

"He attacked me for no reason," he started to say but Keith interrupted.

"That thing pretended to be a fucking woman. I took off the clothes and saw a fucking dick." He screamed to the cop. Both cops looked at him with sympathy in their eyes, both wanting to let him loose so he could finish the job.

"I want to press charges," the he/she cried while trying to cover up his body.

"Shut up before we let him go," one of the officers said to him while still attempting to calm Keith down. Keith released the alcohol and his dinner all over the floor. His mind was in a twisted place. He'd let a man suck his dick. He was thoroughly disgusted. Murder was on his mind. All he wanted to do was kill the dude and erase the night from his memory, permanently.

The officers walked Keith to the hallway for a private chat.

"Look, we understand how you feel. With that being said, we aren't going to charge you with a damn thing. As much as we want it, we can't let you to continue to pulverize the guy. We will call you a cab and let you leave if you promise not to go looking for this POS. I'd say you got adequate revenge on him." The first officer said to him.

"You messed him up pretty damn bad. We are going to have to call the paramedics for him. Take our advice and go on home and try to forget about this fucked up shit." The second one added. Keith looked at them both, contemplating his options. As much as he would like to murder the POS, he knew he couldn't act out on his urges. His son didn't deserve to have a father stuck in prison for killing someone. And plus, this whole sordid affair would be splashed everywhere. He wanted this shit to go away, never to be relived again unless it was by him. He made his choice. He accepted the advice of the officers, got in the cab, took his ass home. At home he scrubbed his body over and over until he was red and irritated. He poured mouthwash over his penis. After all that, he grabbed a bottle of E&J and got twisted out of his mind. He didn't wake up until four in the afternoon the next day.

As soon as the night before flashed in his mind, he ran to the bathroom and took another steaming hot shower. The images were replaying over and over. His resolve snapped as he fell to his knees and sobbed. He couldn't believe the way his life had turned out in the past few months. It went from sugar to shit in a matter of minutes. What messed him up the most was that he had very little control of the things that were taking place in his life. It was as if it all was happening to someone else and he was a spectator to it all. He found himself praying to God for the strength to carry on and get himself on track, to find a way to get his family back and keep them there. He prayed for the safe return of both Leslie and his son, Mason.

Chapter 22

It had been a few days since Leslie had spoken to her best friend. She missed Darcy and Bre like crazy. All she did in Columbia was work and take care of her son. Hanging out no longer appealed to her and her trust in people was limited. There was always a risk in calling home. Everyone attempted to get her to come home or find out exactly where she was. She wasn't ready for unexpected guests and she knew that if she let it be known then someone would eventually tell Keith. Her thoughts settled in on him and how happy they were before he cheated.

He was her true love, her heart, she adored everything about him and he had to go and ruin it for a quick nut. Leslie picked up her phone and dialed Bre. She needed to hear a friendly voice.

"Hello," Bre answered on the third ring. Leslie heard her breathing hard and wondered what it was she interrupted her friend doing.

"Hey lady, how are you?" Leslie said into the phone.

"Leslie, girl, what's going on with you?" Bre's voice rose with excitement.

"Nothing much, I was sitting here thinking about you guys. How have you been doing?"

"You know me, I do enough just to get along." Bre's laughter made her smile for the first time that day. She really did miss her girlfriends.

"You are still crazy as ever. I miss you guys so much. So, what exactly did I catch you doing because I hear you over there breathing like a dragon and shit." Leslie laughed into the phone. It felt great to finally be able to laugh with her girlfriend again.

"I just got out of the shower, that's my story and I'm sticking to it. And you know what to do about missing us, suga. Bring your ass back home where you belong because we all miss you, especially Keith." Bre slipped that last part in.

"Whatever, Keith is probably shacking up with that skank by now." She pretended as if she wasn't interested in how he was doing on multiple occasions, but on this day, she really needed to know. She had to know. She never allowed them to talk about him before, so they kept his actions to themselves.

"Leslie, Keith isn't doing well at all." The seriousness in Bre's voice peaked her interest tremendously.

"What do you mean?"

"Since you've been gone, all he does is sit in that house and drink. He looks a mess. He doesn't take care of himself anymore."

Leslie's heart constricted with the thought of him hurting like that. "Are you serious?"

Bre took a deep breath before continuing, "Yes and it's so damn sad. If it wasn't for Darcy and me, he probably wouldn't eat and the house wouldn't get cleaned. Sometimes, we even have to make him take a bath. Leslie, he has gone down since you left him. He's broken and we are all worried that he's going to do something crazy eventually."

"Oh my goodness Bre, is it really that bad there?" Leslie's mind started working overtime. As much as he hurt her, she didn't wish harm upon him. He was still Mason's father after all.

"He needs you, Leslie. He needs you now more than ever." Bre informed her, hoping that she would finally be able to get through to her.

"Look, this is a lot to think about. I'll call you back later, okay." She hung up on her friend and sat back with her thoughts. Keith needed her and she was not there for him. She knew what she had to do. She had to return home and help him get his life back on track. Even though it still hurt her to think about him being with another woman, this pain was far worse. The thought of losing him completely had her crying her eyes out. The next day she made the arrangements. She rented a U-Haul loaded Mason up and drove home.

The drive took a little over twenty-four hours. She wished she had the stamina to drive straight through. Since she had her son's safety to consider, she made a few stops along the way. She prayed that Keith wasn't too far gone. No one knew she was on her way home and she preferred it that way. She needed some alone time with Keith without any interruptions from anyone at all. After all, this was between them and not the whole world. When she arrived at the house, she wondered if this was all a ploy to get her back home. Maybe they all had devised this plan to get her here. If so, then she was not going to speak to any of them ever again. Leslie took a deep breath before removing Mason from his car seat. She made sure to get his diaper bag before closing the door.

Keith wasn't answering the door even though she saw his car in the driveway. Remembering where they always kept their spare key, she entered the house, afraid of what awaited her on the other side of the door. The house reeked. She frowned as she saw the state of the place. All of the blinds and curtains were closed and the air was stale. The living room, kitchen, and bathroom were in the worst shape. Mason's room was still the same with not one little thing out of place.

Upon entering their old bedroom, Leslie spotted Keith's form laid out across the bed. She moved closer and called his name. He didn't respond. There was a bottle of Jack Daniels on the stand by the bed. She knew he was passed out cold. With her mind made up, she went in search of his car keys. Loading Mason up in Keith's car, she went to the nearest shopping mart to get food and cleaning supplies. She realized that she would be less than a woman if she left him in this position. Back at the house, she put Mason down for a nap and got started on ridding the place of the stench and garbage.

The cleaning actually took less time than she expected. She opened the windows so the house could air out and she begun to prepare dinner. Her son must have been worn out, his nap lasted a good while. Dinner was almost complete by the time he woke up. She cleaned him up and brought him to the kitchen with her. While sitting at the table, she heard Keith moving around upstairs. The moment of truth had arrived. Would he tell her to leave, she had no clue.

"Darcy, I told you I don't need you coming here trying to take care of me. I'm fine; I just want to be left alone." His voice was coarse as he made sure he was heard. Leslie didn't say anything, knowing the smell of dinner would eventually draw him to the kitchen.

"Damn, it smells good in here," he said as he entered the kitchen. She took in his appearance and her heart shuddered. Her sweet Keith looked worse for wear. He had a nappy afro and nappy facial hair. His shorts were dingy and stained like he hadn't changed them in a while. He had lost some weight. She felt the tears prickling behind her eyelids. She wanted to wrap her arms around him and promise that everything would be okay. She felt the need to protect him and mend his broken heart. Her love for him made coming home easy.

She admitted to herself that she believed they could work out their problems. She was now willing to try and save her family; the family that she'd work so hard on having in the first place. She realized that she knew Keith better than anyone else and in her heart she knew he wasn't a cheater. It wasn't in his character at all.

Not even noticing who it was in the kitchen; Keith went straight to the refrigerator and took out a beer. Without turning to face her he said, "Hey, thanks for going shopping again. I guess I keep forgetting to do it."

"Keith," Leslie called out to him. His hand stilled on the way to his mouth. He stood there rooted in that spot before turning towards her.

"Leslie," he whispered before dropping to his knees. His beer fell to the floor, spilling all of the contents on the freshly mopped floor. Neither one of them paid attention to the mess though. She walked over to him and wrapped her arms around him. He buried his face in her stomach and cried while squeezing her as tight as he could, afraid that she would somehow vanish if he were to release her.

"Keith, I need to get Mason," she told him while cradling his head. At the mentioning of his son's name, his head snapped up and he looked around spotting his son.

"Look at my boy, he's getting so big," he wiped the tears from his face. His smile finally reached his eyes. The dull, glazed look was gone at last.

"Why don't you go get cleaned up and then come back down for dinner." Leslie told him. He looked from her to their son like he wasn't sure if it was wise to leave the room; like they would be gone upon his return to the kitchen.

"We will be here waiting for you, I promise." Leslie smiled at him, reassuring him that they were not going anywhere.

"Okay," he conceded before making his way back up the stairs to shower.

"Well that went better than I expected," she said to her son while continuing to feed him.

She was taking the garlic bread from the oven when Keith returned to the kitchen smelling good and freshly shaven. He had gone through a drastic transformation in a matter of thirty minutes. She was literally surprised at how he had managed to change in that length of time. Clean clothing and freshly shaven, Keith resembled the man she fell in love with. He was almost back to his normal self, except for the weight loss. That was something that she had no qualms that could be fixed in a matter of days. He had a ravenous appetite and she planned on preparing all of his favorites until he regained his former weight.

"I was afraid that I was dreaming," he admitted to her. She saw the nervous twitch in his eyes. He wasn't sure of what to expect from her and she was well aware of that. Her heart went out to him. She ached for the love they once shared. She knew without a doubt he was the man for her, he was meant just for her.

"No dream, we're really here." She felt her face flaming.

"Leslie, baby, you don't know how much I have missed you and our son." He walked over to her and Mason. The longing to hold Mason was strong in his eyes.

"Go ahead and hold him," Leslie smiled at him letting him know that she was alright with it. Instantly, she felt horrible for denying him the chance to be a father. Mason was his world and she took that from him all because of her hurt. Realization set in for her. Even though he was wrong, he didn't deserve all that she'd put him through.

Running away was a selfish move on her part which not only affected her, but Mason and Keith also. Mason was denied access to his father when he did no wrong in the entire situation. She had to make up for all of the lost time between the two of them. Keith was a wonderful father. He was always so attentive to his son's needs. He never considered spending time with his son babysitting like a lot of men did.

His family was home. He was ecstatic. He thought he was waking to another dreadful day. Instead it was the complete opposite. His sweet Leslie had come home to him, bringing his son back. The dark clouds faded instantaneously and a rainbow took their place. Everything he had been neglecting suddenly took precedent again. He needed to get himself back on track and get rid of all the negative energy. He picked up his son noting how much he'd grown since the last time he saw him. He held him close to his chest and breathed in his sweet smell. He felt his eyes watering and his heart slowing mending. Leslie placed a hand on his back and rubbed up and down. He closed his eyes and relished in the love he was experiencing at that time.

"Are you hungry?" She asked him.

"Um, actually, I think I'm starved," he laughed, realizing that he was very hungry. He had been too busy wallowing in self-pity and drinking to take the time out and eat.

"Good because I prepared your favorites. Have a sit and I will fix you a plate." She led him to his chair and he sat down, sit holding on to Mason for dear life.

"What did you cook?" He asked her. He could pick out a few dishes with just the smells alone. He knew for sure that she had made spaghetti. It was his absolute favorite dish ever along with some cheesy garlic bread.

"It's a surprise," she turned and smiled at him while she continued to fix his plate. After she was done, she placed his food in front of him. "Why don't you hand me Mason and dig in?" She took their son and placed him in his highchair. Then she brought her and Mason's plate to the table to join Keith for their first family dinner in months.

"Would you like to say grace?" He asked Leslie.

"Yes, I would," Leslie blessed the food and they had a nice quiet dinner with each of them glancing at one another wanting to be in the other's arms, but trying to take things slow. The longer they sat there, the more his temperature rose. He needed to feel her in his arms, her lips on his. Upon finishing his food, he stood and walked over to Leslie. He took her by the hand, pulling her from her chair and into his arms. She wrapped her arms around him as he placed his face in her neck and inhaled. His hold tightened around her waist.

"My baby, God, how I've missed you," his breath tickled her neck. She'd missed those arms of him more than anything else in the world. He had always made her feel safe and secure.

"I've missed you also," she finally admitted to him and herself at the same time. There was no longer a reason to fight it any longer. She was home to stay if he would have her. The time apart from him was horrible. Leslie had no desire to continue on with their separation. She wanted Keith back. She needed Keith back in her life for herself and for Mason. They all belonged together.

"Tell me what to do to make this better because I can't take being without you guys. That's not the life I want. I can't breathe without you, baby." He looked deep in her eyes and continued, "I'm so sorry for what I did, for hurting you. I fucked up bad and I need to know how to fix it? I need you home with me where you belong." He pleaded with her.

"All of that is no longer necessary," she began.

"What do you mean," his body froze in place. His thought automatically flew to Leslie leaving again. The parts of his heart that was slowly mending begin pulling apart again.

"I mean I'm not living in the past any longer. From this moment forth, we live for today. I can't be without you any longer, Keith. I love you so damn much and I don't..." she was no longer able to speak as the tears flowed freely. Keith held her face in his hands as he kissed her tears away.

"Oh Leslie, baby," he groaned. He brushed his lips across hers before settling in with a soul searching, toe curling kiss.

Leslie

"Dinner's ready," she said as she piled food on his plate. She was here to get him back where he needed to be and that meant helping him build his body back up. He gave Mason a kiss and placed him back in his high chair before sitting down in front of his plate. Leslie sat in her old spot and said grace before they started eating. They made small talk through out their meal and moved to the living room once they were done cleaning the kitchen. The nervousness that she had felt was slowly receding. The laughter came easily and when he pulled her onto his lap, she automatically placed her head on his chest.

"Leslie, my love, I'm sorry for every little thing I did to cause you pain. I apologized for destroying our family. You are the love of my live, my comfort, my everything. Without you I am nothing, without you is not a place I want to be. I will do anything that I can to make this right. All I ask is that you please allow me the chance to do so. I miss you and

Mason more than anything in this entire world. Baby, I need you both to survive." She wiped the tears from his face. Her handsome man was completely broken and she had the power to repair the damage if only she could learn to forgive him completely. She wasn't sure if they would be able to return to the way things were before, but she was going to give it a shot.

"I love you too, Keith. I want us to make this work. I want to move back in." She whispered. He held her face in his hands and looked in her eyes before leaning down to capture her lips. It had been too long since she'd experienced the touch of another person outside of Mason. Kissing Keith had always been one of her most favorite things. His lips were always sweet, kisses were always deep. He always knew right where to touch her to make her lose control. She let him lead her to their bedroom and remind her of all that she was missing. He showed her how much he wanted her. He loved her in ways that only he knew how to do. Leslie's mind was preoccupied for the rest of the night until the wee hours of the morning. Keith kept her busy. Keith kept her wet. Keith kept her cumming over and over again until she literally begged him to allow her time to recuperate.

Chapter 23

It was a glorious day to be alive. Keith woke with a huge smile on his face. For the first time in months, he was looking forward to the day. It had been a long time since he'd waken up without a hangover. He felt energized and it was all thanks to the woman that was snuggled up next to him with her head on his chest. He pulled her closer to him and placed a kiss on top of her head. Her curly hair was loose and wild, just like he liked it. He said a quick prayer, thanking the man above for allowing his family to return to him. He knew they had a long road ahead of them, but he was more than ready for the task. His family was more than worth it.

"Um mm, good morning," Leslie yawned and stretched her body in a similar fashion as a cat does.

"Good morning, beautiful." Keith said while running his fingers through her hair. His eyes roamed over her body, taking in all of her delicious curves that he had the pleasure of familiarizing himself with all over again.

"I could stay like this all day." Leslie sighed and wiggled closer to him. She felt him hardening against her bottom. Her body responded instantaneously. The throbbing between her legs started slowly, gradually growing with the more contact between them.

"We can," Keith wanted to make her comfortable and happy. He especially wanted to keep them to himself for a little while longer. He knew once everyone found out they were home, the phones would be ringing off the hook with people wanting to visit and her friends wanting to hang out. All he wanted was some much needed alone time with his family. They had a ton of work to do on their relationship which was best done between the two of them and not the whole community.

"Good because I'm not ready to deal with people right now." She admitted to him. He was surprised that she felt the same exact way as he did about the situation.

"So what would you like to do? We can bring Mason in here and lounge in the bed all day." He suggested to her. His fingers were making slow trails on her skin while he spoke. Her voice started to quiver when she talked. He knew what he was doing to her body, she was sure of it. He had always had the ability to make her lose her train of thought and bring her body to life at the same time.

"How about if we just go with the flow?" She didn't care at the moment. All she wanted was to feel him inside of her loving her, kissing her, and whispering sweet nothings in her ear.

"That will work." His hand slipped down to cup her bottom and he gave it a gentle squeeze. "Right now I think I need to familiarize myself with your body some more." He told her before tilting her head to grant him easy access to her neck.

"I'm quite sure you did that last night," she moaned as his lips made contact with her skin. Her body was on fire with that one kiss.

"I need a whole day to do it, Leslie. You know me, I have to kiss and caress every inch of your luscious body." He rolled her over onto her back and climbed on top of her. "Any objections lady,"

"None," she cried as he nibbled on her breast. His Leslie was home and he was damn sure going to get his fill of her before allowing others to invade their time and home.

***

Leslie had been home for a total five days. She and Mason were strictly his for five whole days without interruptions from any outside people. During that time they had heart to heart talks. They bonded as a family. It had been the best time ever, but it was time for him to return to work. He had his family back; it was definitely time to get back on the right track at work. He had people depending on him. Leslie was already talking of looking for work, but Keith told her to wait it out for a while, just to see how it all played out.

He'd rather have her home taking care of Mason. She agreed with him and he was ecstatic that she granted him her trust and allowed him to make a major decision like that. That was all the more reason for him to get everything back on track, even if it meant working some overtime and doing some major kissing up. He was thankful that he still had a job after the way he'd behave the last few months. His suspension was the final straw before the big bosses were going to toss him out on his ass. Now, he was going to work all of that shit off of his record and get back on top of his game. He had his mojo back. His number one cheerleader had returned. The game was on lock and he was in it to win it.

Upon his return to work, his coworkers were surprised to see him in such a good mood. He spoke to all he came in contact with. His smile was as bright as the sun and his eyes sparkled. He tackled his work with gusto. He buried himself in his office, attempting to catch up on most of the work that he had been neglecting. He was quite certain he wouldn't be able to get it all done in one day. It would be a miracle if he caught up within one week, but he was damn sure going to try. He knew it would be worth it in the end when he'd be able to spend more time at home with his family.

Keith was buried in his work when he heard a knock on the door. He was hesitant for a second before calling out to the person to enter. He was surprised when the CEO of the company walked in and took a seat across from him.

"I'm glad to see you are feeling better. For a while there, I thought we were going to have to let you go." The man said with a smile on his face.

"I apologize for my insubordination. I was in a bad place mentally and I didn't know how to shake it off." Keith admitted to his boss. Now that Leslie was back, he could be upfront about how losing Leslie affected his life.

"Well, whatever happened, I'm thankful for it."

"My love came home. I have my family back. Leslie and Mason are my world and I finally have them back and I won't make the same mistake again." Keith's eyes held determination as he spoke with the man. His dedication to his family was evident to the older gentleman and he respected Keith for accepting his faults and working to make things better. He stood and stuck out his hand for Keith to shake.

"Congratulations on the return of your family. Make sure you take care of them. Do what you have to, to make your family strong. There's nothing more important to the growth of a man. Family is everything." He said to Keith before exiting his office. Keith sat back in his chair to think about what the man said. His family was his everything and it was more than time to put them first. He learned a painful lesson and he was ready now. Partying and all of that only led to trouble. He'd rather be home with his loved ones instead. He sat back in his chair as images of the last year played out in his mind. If he could, he would go back in time and kick his own ass for messing up the best thing that ever happened to him in his whole entire life.

Chapter 24

Leslie was lying on the couch while the baby was napping in his playpen when Keith got home from work. They had spent the day flirting with one another via text messages. For lunch, she surprised him by showing up at his office for a midday snack which he took to mean feasting on her body. Her afternoon had her so elated that when he proposed, she didn't hesitate to accept it. The surprise was evident in his voice when he asked if she was sure. She laughed as she told him that with him is where she was always meant to be. She knew he still had doubts and worries about her up and leaving him again, but she tried to prove to him that as long as he did what he was supposed to do they would be together, but if he fucked up again, then there would be no going back, no repairing their relationship.

One of those silly talk shows was going on full force when she heard his car pulling up in the drive-way. Her heart skipped a beat even though she'd seen him less than four hours ago. To her it felt like the way it was when they first started seeing one another. The anticipation of his kiss had her body tingling with upcoming desire. Her inner freak was rearing her head. She was more than ready to explore and take things to the next level with Keith. She just hopped that he was prepared and open-minded to her suggestions.

"Hey baby," he called out as he entered. He took off his shoes, removed his jacket, undid his tie and climbed on top of her to give her a kiss.

"Hey you," she replied after their kiss ended. Images of her tied to the bed, blindfolded, with him standing over her with a flogger floated in and out of her imagination. She bit her lip as the impact in her mind made her jump slightly. He didn't seem to notice it though.

"Are you sure you're ready to marry me?" He placed a kiss on her neck. He was still surprised that she'd said "yes" that quickly. He just knew she was going to tell him they needed more time.

"Yes, I said I was." She laughed and he tightened his arms around her.

"I know what you said, I want to be sure. Don't want you to feel pressured." His hands started roaming over her body, taking his time, caressing her curves.

"Keith, stop it," she moaned against his cheek.

"Oh no, I can't. I've been thinking about this all day." He moaned against her throat.

"You just had some at lunch, remember." She giggled, delighted by his appetite for her.

"And I want more. I have some making up to do lady. Besides, you shouldn't feel so damn good." He pushed her shirt up to reveal her breasts. At the sight of them, his mouth watered. He lavished kisses all around her nipples before taking one of them in his mouth.

"Keith," she moaned, spreading her legs wider to allow him greater access to his treasure. Being without his touch all of those months was pure torture to her body. It craved his touch and his sweet kisses.

"I knew you would see it my way." He turned his attention to her other breast. Their son made a noise and he stilled and waited to see if he was going to wake up. When he didn't, Keith continued with his magical tongue.

"The baby might wake up," she pleaded with him.

"Then I'll make it quick." He wasn't giving up. He wanted to feel her. He was just about to pull her short off when someone ranged the door bell. They were planning on ignoring it, but then the person pounded on the door.

"Shit," Keith exclaimed as he got up to go to the door. He attempted to arrange his rock hard dick in his pants before opening the door. Leslie laughed at his struggles because his boner was a tad bit too large to hide.

"I'm going to put him in his room." Leslie said as she scooped up the baby before the knocking woke him up. Keith looked back and rolled his eyes at her for laughing at his discomfort. Before making her way upstairs, she heard the voices of Sam and Telvin.

"**D**ude, what's good with you? I've been calling you for the last week! Why the hell haven't you answered your damn phone?" Sam fussed at Keith as he pushed his way past him on into the house. They entered the kitchen and sat down on the bar stools. He shook his head in amazement. Just when he thought it was all clear to get freaky with his baby, they had to interrupt their flow.

"I've been busy lately," he told his friends. This was the truth because he and Leslie were working on repairing their relationship. He hadn't been concerned with reassuring them that he was straight after the last time that he had spoken with them. He knew they had been worried about him for a while. But he was finally in a good place; Leslie had made sure of it. He had his family back and he was on his way to making her his wife. What he really needed at that time was for them to leave as soon as possible because whatever they had to say had nothing on what he knew was waiting upstairs for him.

"Man, you've been locked up in this house drinking your damn life away. Do you really think that you are ever going to get her back like this?" Sam argued. Keith opened his mouth to tell him about Leslie, but Telvin cut him off.

"Sam is right. The last time I saw you, you looked a damn hot ass mess. I'm glad you cleaned your ass up for work. Man, you have got to get it together because," Telvin stopped talking when Leslie entered the kitchen.

"Hey Sam and Telvin," she spoke to each man as she walked over to the sink to wash out Mason's bottle, knowing they were watching her each and every move. Keith knew she had done it on purpose just to let them know that their little intervention was not necessary. They were riding his ass hard, not giving him the chance to respond to anything they said. He attempted to hide his laughter at the look on both of their faces. Yeah, he was definitely winning again and their faces more than proved it!

153

"Hey Leslie," Sam replied with disbelief written all over his face. Keith smirked at both of his friends. He walked up behind her and asked her if the baby was still sleeping. She told him yes then turned to leave the room, but not before Keith had a chance to grab a handful of her butt. She squealed with delight as she swatted his hand away.

Keith turned to his friends and said, "Look, I appreciate you guys checking up on me but as you can see, I'm good, I'm really good. But I need y'all to leave right now because my son is sleep and my future wife is waiting on me. So thanks for the visit but duty calls." He said while ushering them to the door. "I'll call you later on." He called out to them before closing the door and heading upstairs taking those two at a time.

He eased their bedroom door open and saw Leslie on the bed completely naked. She was putting on a show for him. He stripped his clothes off on his way to the bed. He watched her playing with herself for a little bit. When she was about to raise her hand to her mouth, he reached out and placed those same fingers in his mouth instead.

"Mine," was all he said as he slurped the juices from her fingers. Leslie's body was on fire and he knew it. It didn't take long for him to make her cum with his tongue. Once he was inside of her, she demanded him to go faster and harder. She was begging him to take her there and he gave her all that she wanted, all that she needed. His body moved in tune with hers as they made sweet love which seemed to get better by the day. He held her close as they floated back down to earth. His world was back on track and he'd be damned if he allowed another person to come between them again. He was meant to be with Leslie for the rest of his life and that's what he was going to do by any means necessary.

Chapter 25

Leslie was glad she made the decision to return home. If she was honest with herself, she'd missed Keith and the life they shared tremendously. She vowed she would attempt at making their relationship work this time around. She needed some serious advice on her life and the predicament she found herself in. There was only one person she trusted to always be honest and offer decent advice. She called her grandmother and made plans to have lunch with her the following day. Leslie wasn't quite ready to return to her normal everyday life. She didn't like the looks of pity people threw her way when they saw her. She was still keeping a very low profile.

Leslie's grandmother pulled her inside the house and hugged her and Mason at the same time.

"I'm so glad to see you baby," she cried, still holding them tight.

"I'm glad to see you, Big Ma," Leslie felt tears burning her eyes. She'd missed this woman, tremendously, while she was away even though she did call her quite often.

"How is everything going with Keith?" The older lady asked her while leading her to the kitchen to sit.

"It is great, really great actually. I wish we could have had a few more days of complete privacy, but I know he has to work." Leslie admitted to her.

"Oh, I can understand that. It's like when you first started dating all over again, right?" Her question was right on point with Leslie's thinking.

"Yes, I didn't think it was possible to love him more than I did at first. Now, it's different, more intense. I can't really explain it, but he has changed."

"So have you, that's why it's more. You both have grown over the last few months. You had to do without one another. Y'all had to grow and find your places in life which neither one of you liked much when y'all were apart. Now that you are back together, y'all are willing to work harder on keeping your relationship. The time apart has made you both a lot stronger."

"Thanks for the advice. I can't really explain how I'm feeling at the moment. I just want him near me at all times." Leslie said as she took a sip of her tea. Mason was having a field day with the slice of bacon on his plate.

"So, when will I have another baby to spoil?" Grandma asked her as Leslie's cheeks turned red. "Girl, I don't know why you are so shame faced. It ain't like I don't know what's going on between couples. Y'all already got one kid." She shook her head and chuckle at her granddaughter. She knew Leslie was a soft-hearted person through and through. Leslie spent another hour with her before heading home to start dinner. She still hadn't called her girlfriends and let them know she was back. To be completely honest, she was more than surprised that Sam and Telvin had managed to keep quiet about. She decided she'd call them and make plans to meet up on the weekend. Well of course if Keith was cool with it. Maybe they all could do something together like they used to. She missed them hanging out all of the time. Her relationship with Keith caused the strain amongst them all. That wasn't fair to the others. She and Keith had some serious work to do to repair the bond between the six of them.

Before returning home, she decided to go to the movie store and pick out a couple of DVDs for them to watch if he wasn't too tired when he got home. What she really wanted to do was head over to the new novelty store and pick out a few items. She didn't think it wise to go inside with her son, so she chose to bypass it making a mental note to stop by as soon as possible. Maybe she'd end up turning Keith out the same as he'd done her. She smiled at the thought of the look that would grace his beautiful face once she worked up the courage to surprise him. His happiness was all that mattered to her. She knew it was her responsibility to keep her man happy and quite satisfied. Then there would be less chances of another woman sneaking in to seduce her man. And Keith was that, her man, the father of her son, her soon- to-be husband. The man she loved more than anything in this world, well besides her son. They were running neck and neck in the race.

Chapter 26

Bre, Darcy, and Leslie were finally hanging out on a Saturday night without the guys. After much negotiation, Leslie let them convince her she needed a night out. They knew she wasn't too fond of club hopping. So, they settled on dinner and a movie. They parked downtown at a garage and walked the rest of the way. It had been a while since Leslie walked through her city. She missed the excitement of mixing with people of all ages and backgrounds. They walked over to the cinema to catch a movie. They were sitting at an outside table of a prominent restuarnat when Ashlyn spied them. They weren't aware they were being watched.

"Hey ladies, what's going on over here? I see I missed my invitation to hang out with my girls.

Leslie's head whipped around at the sound of her voice. Her temper flared. She couldn't believe the bitch had the nerves to approach their table with her sitting there, after almost destroying her relationship with Keith.

"What do you want, Ashlyn?" Darcy asked her without looking up.

"I just saw you ladies out having a fabo time without me. I thought we were all girls." She looked around the table and then her eyes fell on Leslie, "Hey Leslie girl, I heard you moved out of town. When did you get back?" There was a smirk on her face like she knew some sort of big secret that none of them were aware of.

"I've been back for a while now. Why do you want to know?" Leslie asked her. She was itching to call her out for her deception.

"No reason," Ashlyn began to say something else but Leslie held up her hands.

"Yes, Keith and I are back together. No, you will never ever take him from me and if you even think about interfering in our relationship again, I'll make sure to give you something to remember me by." Leslie's eyes held fire as she stared the other woman down. She was ready for something, anything to pop off so she could let out all of the past animosity that she had for Ashlyn.

"What are you…?"
"Bitch don't play. We know what you did. So, if I were you I'd remove myself from this area before you get what's coming to you." Darcy threatened her silently.

"This is a free country. You bitches do not own this shit." Her hands flew to her hips in protest. Leslie jumped up from her seat. She was about to check Ashlyn, but Bre pulled her back just in the nick of time.

160

"Les, you don't want to do this. You are a lady and ladies don't do shit like this. Forget the trash and let's finish with our dinner. You know for a fact that she isn't worth it and Keith doesn't want her ass."

"Yeah, you're right," Leslie agreed before returning to her seat and picking up her glass of water to take a sip.

"Well if Keith didn't want me, why did he have his big dick down my throat?" She questioned her old girlfriend.

"Because you are a whore, a slut. That's the type of shit you do. You caught him while he was weak and drunk. You knew what you were doing and that shit makes you the lowest form of living species there is." Bre finished and turned her attention back to her menu.

"I ain't my fault she wasn't satisfying her man right." She threw in. Leslie stood up and threw the remained of her sweet tea in Ashlyn's face. With a look of pure hatred, she said to the woman, "Stay away from me and my family or I will hunt you down and gut you like the filthy pig you are. You are a waste of space and I'd be more than happy to erase you to make room for someone else." Ashlyn gasped at the words that were coming from the otherwise calm, quiet Leslie.

None of them had ever witnessed her lose her cool before and they were speechless. Ashlyn was the first to recover. She picked up a napkin to dry her face before storming off without saying another word to the women.

"Damn, I did not see that coming," Darcy laughed so loud that other patrons turned in their direction.

"That was some seriously funny shit right there," Bre added while trying to control her urge to laugh.

"Did you see the look on her face? I thought she was going to perish from shock?" Darcy wiped her eyes with a napkin. She had tears streaming down her face.

"It was not that damn funny," Leslie reprimanded her friends. Her raging temper was still in full effect. She so badly wanted to strangle Ashlyn until every bit of life seeped out of her body. Her control had slipped, but she was able to reel it back just in time before she did something she'd end up regretting.

She realized that she was going to have a long road ahead of her if she was going to make her relationship with Keith work. Leslie had to determine if what they had was worth fighting for. Ashlyn was trash and she was less than a woman for trying to come between them. But that, she could deal with. It was the other thought that bothered her.

What if Keith experienced another moment of weakness? If he cheated once, would it make it easier for him to do it again? She seriously had to get things in order before she made the wrong choice. It was more than just her and Keith on the line. Their whole livelihood was at risk and all of it could eventually affect their son. She needed to know if with her and Mason is where his heart truly resides. She knew she couldn't suffer through another heart break by his hands. She had to learn how to trust him all over again. No half-stepping this time, it had to be all or nothing. She loved him, but one more fuck up like that and she'd leave him for good. It felt good to be home, but with shit like that happening, she couldn't help but be reminded of all of the things he put her through.

Chapter 27

Keith and Mason were chilling big time while Leslie was out on the town with her friends. He had encouraged her to go hang out just to get out of the house for a while. She'd basically been stuck inside since she'd returned home. He was astounded at the growth of his son. Soon he probably would be walking and talking to boot. He was more than ready to take him out on the basketball court and teach him how to play ball. He simply adored being a father to such a wonderful son. Keith heard his phone alerting him of an incoming message. He picked up the device wondering if one of his boys was hitting him up. To his surprise, it was from Leslie.

Leslie:

I just had the pleasure of seeing your bitch.

Keith's heart skipped a beat. If Leslie was some how reminded of what went on between the two of them, would she consider leaving him again? He felt the terror seeping in his bones.

Keith:

Baby, what are you talking about?

He knew it was a stupid reply, but he didn't know what to do or say at the moment.

Leslie:

Keith don't play. I just saw Ashlyn and she reminded me of how big your dick is and how she had it all down her throat.

"Fuck," Keith cried out. Ashlyn was fucking things up in a major way. The shit she had just done was not cool in the least bit. He was going to have to put her ass in check and make it all up to Leslie before things continued and got beyond his control. Just then another message came through on his phone. He looked at the number and shook his head. He was afraid of what she'd say this time.

Leslie:

I know we are supposed to be past this but the shit still hurts as much as it did then.'

Keith needed her to come home. He needed to hold her in his arms and let her know that every little thing was going to be fine. He needed to prove to her that it was all about them. So, he told her as much in his message

Keith:

Baby, come home.

Leslie:

I'm still with my girls. I'll be home later on.

Keith:

Baby, please come home right now. I need to see you and talk to you

Leslie:

You can do that once I get there. I'll be home when I'm done.
Keith:
I know that but I want you here with me right now. I'm missing you, my love.
Leslie:
The girls aren't ready to call it a night yet.
Keith:
I understand that but we need to talk, seriously.
Leslie:
About what
Keith:
You and I because I don't want you trying to leave me over some shit she did.
Leslie:
OK, I'll be home as soon as I can. Will that work for you?
Keith:
Yeah, I'll be waiting.
Keith:
And baby, please don't take too long. I really want to see you.
Leslie:
Okay Keith

Keith tossed the phone on the table and put his head in his hands. He prayed that things were not beyond his control. He hoped that Leslie wasn't going to attempt to pull away from him and their relationship. After putting his son to bed, he braced himself for the confrontation he knew was about to happen as soon as she walked in the house. He was sitting on the couch nursing a drink and listening to some slow ole school R&B music when he heard her car pulling up. He had the lights on low as he awaited her entrance. Leslie placed her purse on the chair across from the sofa where

Keith sat. Her eyes held his as she stood rooted to the same spot.

"I missed you," he said to her, breaking the silence between them.

"I wasn't gone for that long." She replied while her eyes remained on him.

"I know, but I still missed you baby. We haven't really spent any time together today." He knew he sounded whiny but he couldn't help it. She was his love and he didn't need anyone trying to come in between them and messing up what they were working on restoring.

"Well, you have me now." She held her hands out in submission. That spoke volumes to Keith. Her submission told him that she was not letting the interference from Ashlyn affect their present relationship. He placed his drink on the table and stood up. He took his time in making his way over to Leslie. His eyes roamed over her face before landing on her soft, full, lips. She'd applied a fresh coat of lip gloss before entering the house, he could tell from the shine of them. He leaned in close to her and inhaled. Her fragrance washed over him and heightened his senses.

Devouring her flashed in his mind before his mouth descended to hers. She kissed him back with a fierceness that surprised the hell out of him. He could tell she was hungry for his love. Her mouth was greedy and very demanding. Her kisses were still the sweetest that he had ever had the pleasure of tasting. His hands flew around her body, pulling her closer to him. He gripped her ass and raised her up then let her slide down his manhood. He heard her gasp when their bodies connected. She wanted him, he could tell. His mind was primal and he wanted to lay claim to her body as he was sure she wanted to do the same to him. There was a static in the air as they continued kissing. Finally, pulling away to catch his breath, Keith leaned his forehead to hers, "I love you and only you," he saw the love in her eyes, her words were not necessary at this point. His fear of her leaving him evaporated the moment their lips touched. Leslie was still his to love and to hold forever.

"Make love to me, Keith." She pleaded. As soon as the words were spoken, all thoughts of anything besides Leslie were no longer present in his mind. His hands were everywhere and his mouth was on hers. Still, he couldn't get enough. He craved more, he needed more. Leslie was in his senses and that was all that mattered to him at that particular moment in time. He felt her hands caressing his head and sliding down to his arms as his grip on her ass tightened.

Her head fell back and he trailed kisses down her throat. Her quick intake of breath had him exploring every inch of skin that was visible. Her skin was soft and delicious. Her smell was intoxicating. His mind was in a fog as she broke away from his hold and slid down in front of him. Leslie undid his pants slowly while gazing up at him. Once he was free, her soft hands began to glide up and down over his erection. Her gaze was full of hunger as she licked her lips. At the sight of her pink tongue darting out between her lips, Keith's dick jumped in her hands. He was already anticipating feeling the warmth of her mouth wrapped around him. His eyes rolled back in his head once she finally placed him in her mouth. He knew he wouldn't be able to last long.

"Oh baby," he moaned. His hands flew to her head and he grabbed handfuls of her hair while thrusting in her mouth. She allowed him to control the moment and let him go as deep as he wanted. He loved the way she had control over her gag reflex. He was able to push deep down in her throat without worrying about her trying to stop him and that shit drove him crazy. She was, by far, the best he'd ever had in his whole lifetime.

"Leslie, uh…baby," he could barely form a complete sentence. She continued her blow job as he tried pulling away. He was about to nut and he wasn't ready for it yet.

"Unh, unh," she moaned around his dick which brought him closer to the finish line. He was attempting to withdraw himself from her mouth but she held on to him and continued until he released his seed. She drank every drop of him while he was almost faint. Once she finally released her hold on him, he fell to the couch. His breathing was erratic and his heart was beating out of control.

"Wow," was all he managed to say.

"Did you enjoy that?" She asked him, knowing quite well that he did. He took in the smirk on her face and smiled.

"I don't know. I think I need another demonstration." He laughed as she punched him in the arm. He pulled her on top of him and held her close. "I love you so damn much, Leslie."

"I love you too, Keith." She said as she straddled his lap. The warmth from her body had Keith growing hard instantly. His desire for her surprised even him. He was hungry and he wanted all she had to offer. The rest of the night was spent with him showing her just how much he craved her, how much he loved her. Keith was thoroughly surprised at his stamina for that night. Before drifting off to sleep, he knew he was going to have to have at least two days of recovery time because Leslie gave as good as she got and that was definitely saying something.

Chapter 28

Three months back at home left Leslie feeling like a brand-new woman. There was a smile on her face each and every day, Keith made sure of that. Mason was thriving, growing like a weed and enjoying time with his father. Keith's weight had improved drastically over that time. All was going well and the wedding plans were coming along accordingly. Leslie convinced Keith they should have a small wedding with only close family and friends in attendance. He agreed to her plans.

He told her that anything she wanted he would agree because that day belonged to her and he wanted it to be exactly as she wanted. Leslie hadn't had any run-ins with Ashlyn since she threw that drink in her face. And that surprised her, she figured that the woman would try and get her payback. Instead, she had managed to leave them be and move on with her life minus Keith. She even made it a point to dedicate one day a week to host their friends' night like they did before Keith and she were a couple. Once the gang was all back together, things progressed smoothly. It was like living in the past. They had drinks, joked, played games, and just enjoyed one another's company. It was a release from being a serious adult all week long. Their time together, they could all let loose and be free of the hassles that came with everyday life.

"I think we should look into getting some horses." Keith said to her one day while they were sitting out on the front porch.

"What are you talking about?" Leslie asked as she took a sip of her sweet tea.

"Raising horses, Arabians to be more specific," He informed her.

"Do you know anything at all about horses?" She inquired, looking amused.

"Sure I do, remember my dad lives on a farm with a few horses."

"I forgot all about that. You are serious aren't you?"

"Definitely, we can start with one mare and five acres. I've been looking for land recently."

"I see you've given this a lot of thought."

"It would be a great investment for our children's future, something that can be passed down generations to come." He was getting excited just from talking about the prospect of it.

"Okay, we can work on doing this. How much are we looking at as far as start-up costs go?"

"Um around five grand which I already have put up just waiting for me to do something with. We can go look for some land next week if you want." He was ready to get started as soon as possible. He thought that maybe if things worked out like he expected, this could turn out to be his future job, future career. No more punching a clock at the office from nine to five and breaking his back for nothing.

"You will have to teach me as we go because I am lost as far as horses go. Well even as far as buying land too." She admitted to him without hesitation. She never thought about owning horses. This could be a new venture for them as a family. Something that they could grow and build and make it an heirloom for their children. It was past time for him to stop thinking in the now and start making big plans for the future. He'd never thought of following in his father's footsteps until lately. While growing up, he couldn't wait to map out his own future, but now, he honestly could say that he admired his father and his drive to make life better for his family.

He always taught Keith right from wrong and helped him become the man he was today. His father never let him slip into that role of a partying teen even though he did get a little outrageous during his college years. That was something he'd tried like hell to keep from his dad. Which he still eventually found out about to his dismay; Keith realized that he wasn't safe from his father's need to meddle in his life. He knew beyond a shadow of a doubt that he was well on his way to becoming just like his father. He smiled to himself thinking about the future and how he hoped to raised his children.

Working on a horse farm would be a great experience for them all as a family. He just hoped that Leslie was completely on board with the ideal. Actions always spoke louder than words and she was in for a surprise when she discovered how much work would go into taking care of the beasts. He was excited at the prospect of teaching his own children how to ride. A life away from the hustle and bustle of the city might be what the doctor ordered for his family. Once he set his mind to something, he usually devoted his time and energy into doing it right. It was just a matter of time before his plan took on roots.

Chapter 29

Keith took the day off from work to get the ball rolling on looking for some horses to purchase. After and excruciating day of attempting to bargain his way through an awesome deal, he was at home having a much needed beer. He'd fell head over heels in love with the animals on first sight. Two was all he was looking to buy, but upon seeing them, he went ahead and splurged on four. Leslie convinced him in getting the other two if he felt it was in their best interest. He shook his head. He still was amazed at the way she'd adjusted to this big change in their lives.

She was game tight for it all, working extra hours helping him get things in order, his backbone of course. Turning on the television, Keith wondered if he'd be able to catch a new episode of The First 48 Hours. He loved that show, but reruns were taking over. It lost its appeal when you'd seen one episode more than three times. He was just starting to get into the show when his cell went off. Thinking it was

Leslie, he didn't even check the caller id before answering, "Hey baby," there was a slight pause before a male voice came through the line shocking the hell out of him.

"Um hello, I'm trying to reach a Keith Lawson." The person on the end of the line stammered.

"This is he, how can I help you?" Keith asked with curiosity laced in his voice.

"Sir, your name was given to us by one of our patients as one of their sexual partners." The person on the other end of the line stated.

"Um, okay, what is this about?" Keith asked

"We need you to come into the office so that we can explain the situation with you in details." The nurse told him in that no-nonsense tone she had. Keith agreed and the woman set up an appointment for him to come in the very next day. When Keith went into the office, what he heard next almost gave him a heart attack.

"I'm sorry that we are meeting like this, but one of my patients was just found to be HIV positive and listed you as a sexual partner. It is imperative that we test you to determine if it was passed on to you." Keith's mind blanked out for a second. It was as if his soul left his body and he was floating around the room. He heard the doctor talking but he didn't comprehend the words that were coming out of his mouth. HIV? His thoughts went straight to Leslie and all of the times he'd made love to her. They were in a committed relationship so they didn't use condoms at all.

"Oh God," he cried out, shocking the doctor momentarily. "I'm supposed to be getting married and I've been having unprotected sex with my fiancé.'

"Please take a deep breath and hear me out. Now, just because your name came up, it doesn't guarantee that you will be positive also. We will run the test and then we can go from there. I suggest you tell your fiancé and have her come in and get tested also just to be on the safe side." The doctor continued on as Keith's heart was breaking all over again. All he could ask was why was this shit happening to him? He had finally got his life back on track only to be thrown a huge ass curve ball. His mind went into overdrive trying to come up with who it was that named him. He hadn't really had sex with anyone since being with Leslie. So, he figured it was before he and Leslie got together. He was wild as hell back in his college days. He and his boys even had the audacity to share women if they were ready and willing to go for it. He knew he was a hellcat back then, but he never assumed that it would come back and bite him in the ass like this. He thought that since it was all mutual, he wasn't hurting anyone.

"Doctor, I'm confused. I'm raking my brain trying to figure out how this is happening. I don't go around having sex with random people and I made it a point to use condoms when I did have multiple partners. And I've been with the same woman for some years now. So, I'm confused, really confused." He put his head in his hands and tried to contain his emotions.

"Well, this is the repercussions of living a double life. You are sitting here talking about how you are about to be married, but you are here for testing because of a man that you'd been with named you as a sexual partner." The doctor looked pointedly at Keith. Keith shook his head back and

176

forth attempting to grasp the man's words. Basically, he'd just accused him of being a down low brotha.

"Excuse me, I'm not fucking gay." Keith's temper was rearing its head. He wanted to wrap his hands around the man's pudgy neck and strangle him.

"A man listed you as his partner, so what does that say about you and your preference?" He held out his hands like everything was obvious. Keith took a deep breath and calmed his nerves. He imagined Leslie sitting next to him, telling him to maintain his composure and get to the bottom of the situation. She would also say that getting mad won't solve a damn thing.

"Okay, so when can I take the test?"

"Right now," the man seemed relieved that Keith had changed the subject of his sexuality.

"If I am positive, would I be able to press charges against the person?" Keith's mind went back to that night in that hotel room after Leslie had taken Mason and left him. He suddenly recalled the dude pretending to be a woman and him almost killing the guy and the police pulling him off of it.

"I don't see how if it was a mutual affair. The person didn't try and keep it from you. They are making sure you are aware of the problem."

"No, you don't understand. I am not fucking gay. My fiancé left me, I was heartbroken, and I went to a fucking bar and got drunk. I left with a woman, a fucking woman. In the hotel room, she was giving me a blow job, but before it could go any further, I found a fucking dick! It was a damn fucking man! I tried my best to kill that motherfucker. The only thing that saved his life was the two cops that pulled me off of it." Keith was huffing and puffing by the time he finished

177

his story. The doctor was sitting at his desk with his mouth hanging open. Keith could tell the man didn't know how or what to say at the moment. "So doc, like I said, if I am positive will I be able to press charges?"

"Um, In this case, I think it would be wise to do that. He tricked you with malicious intent. He pretended to be something that he was not so he deceived you. And it's not likely that you will be positive from that small interaction. We will still do the test just to be on the safe side of things. But now, I'm beginning to wonder if this was some sort of payback. Were you charged that night?"

"No, the cops let me leave. They did ask me if I wanted to press charges against him but I just wanted the whole horrible ordeal to disappear. I tried to block it out of my mind and now it is back at full damn force. Now, I have to go home and tell my baby about all of this shit when we are finally in a good place in our relationship. Now, I have to go and break her heart all over again." Keith cried. In his mind, he felt like he was always causing her pain. He began wondering if it would be best just to let her go instead of constantly hurting her. In his mind, there was no easy way out of the situation. Leslie was going to leave him, he was sure. How could this possibly be happening to him at this point of his life? He had major plans, things to do, moves to make. This was a major kink in all of that. He shook his head, "Some how this, too, shall pass."

Chapter 30

Leslie could tell that Keith had something serious on his mind from the way his shoulders were slumped. His eyes were dull and the smile that she normally saw when he came home was missing on that day. Something had happened to steal his joy. She wasn't so sure that she really wanted to find out what went on. They were finally in a pleasant place; she was not ready for another storm to enter their adobe.

"Hey baby," she said as he walked up to her. He took her hands in his and pulled her to him.

"Leslie, my baby, I love you more than life itself. I never want to hurt you. Baby, I'm sorry for each and everything that I have put you through." His forehead touched hers as she saw a tear escape from his eye.

"Keith, what's wrong? What happened, please talk to me, baby," she begged him. She pulled him to her and put her arms around his neck while he broke down and cried like a baby. They slid down to the floor as she continued to hold him. She still didn't know what was wrong, but the way he was weeping had her shedding tears also.

"Baby," she choked between the sobs, "what happened? You are scaring me."

"Oh baby, I'm so fucking scared too," he finally admitted to her. "Damn, baby, I got a call from a doctor's office stating that one of my old sexual partners had tested positive for HIV." Leslie blood ran cold. Her arms dropped to her side. No, she thought to herself.

"I don't want to hear this," she screamed at Keith as she got up from the floor. He grabbed her hand to keep her from leaving the room before he could explain.

"Leslie please, I need to tell you this. I need for you to hear me out okay," his eyes begged her to stay. She knew she could never walk out on him.

"Okay," she gave in and sank back to the floor next to him. He put his arm across her shoulder and pulled her next to him as close as he could and told her the whole truth about the incident. After he was done, he leaned his head against the wall and closed his eyes. She placed a light kiss on his cheek and caressed his face.

"I love you baby and we will get through this together." She promised him. He opened his eyes to take her in. They held one another's gaze for a while before she took his face in her hands and kissed him from her heart and soul.

"Thank you for loving me," he whispered to her once their kiss ended. "I promise I'm not gay. I never had any desire to be with a man. And I have not been inside of another woman since I've been with you. All I want is you, baby." His admission tore at her heart. She wished she had the power to make this whole, ugly situation vanish without a single trace. But first of all, she was going to get tested as soon as possible. Even though the chances of them being positive were slim, they would take this as a sign for future references. She thought to herself about all of the obstacles being thrown their way and she knew that with Keith must be where the man above wanted her to be. Otherwise, they wouldn't have to jump all of the hurdles that life had been dishing out for them as a couple. She never once felt as if Keith was gay. He wasn't even homophobic. She knew his philosophy was, "To each his own" He hardly ever judged people and their chosen lifestyles, he just went with the flow and as long as you treated him with respect, he did the same in return.

"I'm here for you like I know you'd be there if it was me in the same situation." She said. He was already broken and she saw how much this was affecting him. She imagined he felt like his manhood had been stripped away from him by force.

"Leslie, I swear I wanted to kill that motherfucker. I saw it happening in my mind and it probably would have if those cops hadn't come to his fucking rescue."

"The cops?" she asked. That admission was something new to her.

"Yeah, I guess I forgot to mention that. When I found a dick, I started whooping his ass. I didn't stop until the police pulled me off of his bitch ass. Man, you can't understand what went through my head when that shit happened. I swear all I saw was red. But the cops, they were real cool and they let me leave without going downtown because they were just as disgusted as I was. I mean, I don't have anything against homosexuals, but to have it forced on you is some different shit. That was not cool in the least bit." As he spoke, she saw that main vein pop out on his forehead.

Waiting for the results had both Keith and Leslie on edge. Each time the phone rang they glanced at one another with thoughts of it being the doctor. Leslie tried her best not to fault Keith for the situation they found themselves in and she'd been doing a tremendous job of it. She'd even let his few rants go, knowing that he was going through some serious shit for any person to have to deal with. She prayed about it each and every night. He'd taken to wearing a condom when they made love. His reasons were commendable to her. She knew some men wouldn't care as much. They'd probably say some shit like "Well since you might already be infected, there is no point in using a rubber." Thankful that Keith was bred from a different cloth, she made her chose to remain by his side regardless of the outcome. It was beyond his control anyways. Being angry wouldn't alter the results at all. It was in God's hands now.

"Baby, guess what," Keith yelled upstairs.

"What," Leslie cried, racing down the steps clutching her chest. She just knew something bad had happened with the way he was yelling at her. When she rounded the corner and entered the kitchen, she saw him standing there with a huge ass grin on his face.

"Dude, you scared the shit out of me." She fussed at him. He paid her no attention while pulling her to him.

"I just got off the phone with the doctor and I'm good, baby! I don't have fucking HIV!" He exclaimed as he squeezed her. Realizing what his words meant, she looked up at him while tears started streaming down her face. God had answered their prayers. He was clear. The devil hadn't managed to get his claws into them.

"Oh my goodness, Keith, that's wonderful!" She wrapped her arms around his neck and pulled his mouth to hers. After their intimate moment, he looked into her eyes leaving her too stunned for words because of the intensity of his look.

"No more condoms for us," he smirked as she burst with laughter.

"Really Keith, after all of that, you are worried about condoms?" She shook her head while holding her side. He was too much for her, but he was all hers.

Chapter 31

Summertime was in full effect and Keith's game was on point. His team was in the lead. Leslie and Mason were in the bleachers cheering him on. He waved to his family as he jogged to the other end of the court. The smiles on their faces made his pride shoot through the roof. Ten more minutes and the game would be over. He continued playing hard until the buzzer went off. He made his way through the crowd of "congratulations" and "good game" over to Leslie. She was holding Mason on her hip. He wiped sweat from his face before wrapping his arms around the both of them.

"Keith," she cried out in pretend disgust, "you're getting us all sweaty."

"Dada," Mason said, reaching for Keith. He placed a sloppy kiss on his son's face before scooping him up from Leslie.

"At least somebody's happy to see me," he smirked at her. Taking her hand, he walked them to their car and placed

LOVING LESLIE

Mason in his car seat before opening the door for Leslie. He stopped her from climbing in so he could steal a quick kiss. "Damn, I can't wait until you are my wife." More kissed preceded the first before she had the chance to reply.

"Does it really matter? I mean we are already living together and we have a kid." She tilted her head to the side allowing him access to her neck. He accepted the invitation and took what she offered.

"Yes, it does matter. Once we are married, you will be mine, officially. Once we are married, only death can do us part, you will belong to me forever."

"My heart already belongs to you," she moaned. "Now let's get out of here so I can get something to eat. Momma's worked up an appetite cheering for her man."

"And daddy's worked up one performing his sweet little lady." He replied as he helped her in the car. Climbing in the car, he turned and asked what she wanted for lunch. She humped her shoulders and told him to surprise her. With that in mind, he knew his woman had a huge appetite and she had a hankering for BBQ. With that in mind, he decided that they deserved some delicious Rib Crib food. He saw the smile appear on her face when she noticed him pulling in the parking lot of the joint.

"Oh goodness, a man after my own heart." She sighed.

"I'm after more than that, baby." He told her with a wink of an eye. He retrieved their son from his car seat and took Leslie's hand and led his family into the restaurant.

Pride, which was Keith's new favorite word, filled him when he looked around the small booth, in which, his little family sat. His lovely Leslie and his handsome son were hanging on to each and every word he said as he described a new horse he

185

was interested in purchasing. Mason's love of horses surprised him. He thought the tyke would be afraid of them at first, but to his shock he took right on up with them. He should have known since horses were in his blood just like his father. The change of careers had him extremely relaxed. No longer did he have to deal with heavy traffic on his way to the office. No more nosy neighbors attempting to be friendly so they could eventually end up borrowing something. No more noises that plague the city, the sirens, the trains, all of it. It was peaceful in their new home. It was a house filled with love and he was enjoying every little minute of it. Leslie leaned in to wipe some food off of Mason's face. The movement brought Keith's attention back to the table.

"Are you guys ready to head home?" He asked them. Yes, they all enjoyed coming to town from time to time, but leaving was always an instant relief.

"I thought you wanted to hang out a little longer today." Leslie's eyes found his. She blushed lightly once she recognized the look in his eyes. She was always able to read him so well, better than most. So he was sure she knew them leaving was first and foremost on his mind. He wanted to get her home and strip those clothes from her delectable body and devour each and every inch of her. The sooner they go home, the sooner Mason would be sleeping which would work out perfectly.

The little guy always managed to fall asleep during the ride back. He couldn't wait to get home and start working on making another baby with her. Life was good, they were good and he was ready to start adding to their family. He wasn't quite sure how Leslie felt about having more children now. He decided he would ease his way in the conversation once they were home. She was a great mom and he loved being a dad. Plus, he wanted his little girl. A little girl just as gorgeous as her mother with a stellar attitude to match. On the ride home, Leslie broached the subject before he even had a chance.

"I think Mason is lonely." She stated, in her opinion.

"Is that right," he didn't take his eyes from the road.

"Don't you think he should have someone to play with? I mean we are living a good distance from everyone we know. Play dates are getting further out in between. I think you should think about it before ruling it out, especially since I'm no longer working." She glanced at him after pleading her case. A case in which wasn't needed being that Keith wanted the exact same.

"Hmm, I don't know. Let me think on it." He told her while smiling inwardly, knowing full well that he was on board with everything she'd said.

"Why do I get the feeling that you've already given this some thought?"

He chuckled, "I'll admit that I have been thinking about it for a while. I think we're ready to expand our family."

"I couldn't agree more," she laid her head on his shoulder and he wrapped his arm around her.

"I love you, my sweet." He placed a soft kiss on the corner of her mouth.

"I love you more, sweet man of mine." She said while turning to capture his lips fully in a heated kiss filled with passion as they waited for the light to change.

Chapter 32

Leslie and Keith were strolling, hand in hand, through the town square when he noticed the face that haunted his past dreams for a while.

"Fuck," Keith growled inwardly. The sudden noise startled Leslie, making her stop in her tracks and look around at people passing them.

"What," she gasped while clutching her chest. His gaze was trained on something in the distance. She couldn't determine what or who was the object of his attention.

"It's him," he stated, never breaking eye contact.

"Him who," she was lost to what was going on with him at the moment.

"The fucker that pretended to be a woman; the bastard that started that whole HIV bullshit. I should go over there and beat the cowboy shit out of him." His eyes held so much anger that Leslie's shudder was visible.

"It's not worth it, Keith." She reasoned with him. He heard her talking but at the same time his feet were leading him in the direction of the guy. He released his hold on her hand and proceeded to move closer before he felt her tugging on his arm.

"Don't do it, I'm begging you to just let it go. You have too much to lose if you let your anger consume you." Her words began to penetrate the fog in his mind. He slowed his step and eventually came to a complete standstill. Leslie had never steered him wrong and he knew this time was no different.

He took a deep breath and calmed his nerves. Hurting the dude would do no good and being away from his family again was not something he wanted to go through. He focused his attention on his lady and exhaled. He hadn't had the pleasure of seeing dude since that night even though he spent countless hours looking for him to possibly beat him to death. He began to realize that maybe God didn't let him find he guy just for that reason. Then he'd be labeled as a murderer and his family would be lost to him because he would be stuck up under the penitentiary. He was thankful for all of his small blessings that led up to the big ones.

"I'm sorry, babe. You are right. Karma has already bitten him in the ass, so there is no reason for me to do anything. We are clean and that's all that matters." He admitted to her.

"That's right, honey. He's going to suffer for everything that he's ever done to people, including you. All you need to do is keep your head on straight and know that God has this all under control." She looked him in the eyes as she squeezed his arm. At that very instant he was finally able to realized that with God and Leslie by his side he would be able to overcome any and ever obstacle that is thrown his way.

He pulled her to him and held her close, "I don't know what I did to deserve you, but I thank God each and every day that you chose to love me."

"You loved me in return, that's what you did." She admitted to him as they held one another on the crowed sidewalk as the people walked around them. He took her hand and continued on their way, not stopping to give it another thought. They'd been given another chance at happiness and nothing or no one was going to interrupt what they'd worked so hard to repair and build. They were finally in a good place; a place that left no room for negativity. Dusk was setting in and the night was warm with a slight breeze. Music spilled out on the street from a few bars on the strip. Keith wrapped his arms around Leslie pulling her close to his side as they continued on their merry way of a night out on the town.

Epilogue

"**K**eith stop, everyone will be here in a few minutes." Leslie moaned as his lips traced delicate kisses along her collarbone.

"I'll be quick," his breath fanned her in the process. Her lady parts clenched at his words. She shook her head from side to side attempting to maintain control of her desire. Their family and friends were expected to arrive within the next thirty minutes.

"Down boy," she slapped at his roaming hand. A look of hurt passed over his face briefly.

"Aw Les, all I need is a little taste," he whined.

"The kids are awake." Leslie was still amazed at their desire for one another after being together four years and birthing two sons. As it was, her spine tingled with pride knowing that her husband still found her attractive and seemed to never get enough of her loving.

Just as he was about to protest, the first guest arrived.

"Damn," he said while making his way to the door. Leslie followed behind him, stopping in the living room to check on the boys. Mason was still absorbed in an episode of Spongebob, while their new addition, Alex, short for Alexander, was swinging peacefully in his Christmas gift from Keith's parents.

"Where are my grand babies?" Keith's mom called out as soon as she crossed the threshold. Mason suddenly lost all interest in television when he heard her voice ringing out over the house.

"Nanny, what did you bring me?" His eyes pleaded. He knew beyond a shadow of a doubt that she had something for him in that suitcase she called a purse.

"Mason where are your manners?" Keith reprimanded him with a look, "You need to try that all over again, little man."

Leslie held back a smile as her son retreated back in the room and changed his approach.

"Hi Nanny," he smiled at her. She pulled him to her for a long hug.

"Hey baby, how are you today?"

"I'm fine," he looked back at his dad. Keith nodded in his direction letting him know it was okay to proceed." did you bring me a surprise?"

The adults laughed at the exchange while Mason waited patiently until his grandmother dug around in her purse, pulling out a small box and handing it to him with a wink.

After a few hours their house was full to the gills. They all sat around the dining room getting ready to start their Thanksgiving feast. It was the first time Leslie and Keith had hosted a holiday dinner together on their horse farm. True enough, she was hesitant at first about moving from town to the outskirts, but Keith managed to make it work out wonderfully. Their business was thriving and life was good. Better than good, they were happy as a whole. She was thrilled at the friendship that developed between Keith and Derek. They were like long lost brothers separated at birth. Blossom called them aunt and uncle and Mason referred to Derek as uncle also.

At first, she thought there would be tension between the two, but Keith surprised her when he accepted the man into their lives. With the way Derek was watching Darcy, she wouldn't be surprised if he ended up being family for real. She winked at Keith and tilted her head in the direction of his cousin. He caught the look of passion passing between them and smirked at his wife.

This was the first big holiday dinner they hosted and Leslie could tell from the gleam in his eyes that this would not be the last one. She looked around the room once more taking in the smiles on each person's face and her heart filled with joy. She asked herself what more could a woman want when her gaze landed on her husband in time enough to catch him checking her out with a look of pure lust on his face. She smiled secretly at him and answered her own question. She knew exactly what more a woman could want and she was planning on collecting once everyone went to their own homes.

Acknowledgments

First, I give praises to the Lord above for finally allowing me to see the light. I would like to thank all of the people that gave me great advice on making a series. As always, I'm thankful to my babies, D'Andre and Blossom, for believing in me and encouraging me to do my thang. Thanks to my family for all of the love and support. Love both of my sisters; Toya and Dee Mitchell.

To my mother Charlene Manning, I apologize for the bad language(lol), but I'm glad that you are enjoying my work.

To my grandmother Hazel Flowers, you are the rock in our family. We would all be lost without you. Love you much!

Love, peace, and happiness!

Sample:

For the Love of All Things
Chocolate
By
Shemeka Mitchell
Coming December 2014

Nicole

I can't believe I slept with my boss! How am I supposed to interact with him at work tomorrow? I dropped down on the couch and took a deep breath. For the life of me I can't even explain how things got out of hand. All I know is we were working on the latest project and the next he had my body pinned against the wall ravishing my mouth with a vengeance. I shuddered at the images playing in my mind. No doubt about it, my boss is drop dead gorgeous. His dark brown curly hair begged for fingers to be run through the curls. His skin was dark, hinting at an Italian heritage with eyes changing between gold and green depending on his mood. My boss hardly ever smiled. He was a terror to anyone in the office. He played no games and was strict as hell. In his line of business he had much respect. There weren't many willing to take him on. He was a shark and he was always out for blood. That's what makes this whole thing so unbelievable. His private life is just that, private. He is hardcore with no plans of settling down. He was never photographed with the same woman who led people to believe he was a playboy, a heartbreaker. With his looks, he could definitely get away with almost anything. Most of the pictures I saw of him and his dates resurfaced. I'm nowhere near in the same league as the women he paraded around. That's why I'm shell-shocked about what took place in his office. I've never dated outside of my race, never really considered it even though I've lusted after good-looking men of all backgrounds. But with Lance, I didn't have a choice in the matter. He acted and I reacted. He gave and I received. And oh boy, what an experience it was. All that hoopla about white men having a small package was in no way true. Lance was hung, well hung. The biggest I've had. Plus, he knew exactly what he was doing when he buried himself deep within me. Just thinking about it had me growing moist all over again.

Lance

"**I** fucked up today." I said to my one and only friend, Shawn.

"What happened, man?" He asked me as he took in my expression. I tried schooling my looks but failed miserably.

"I fucked my employee in my office." I admitted to him. Shawn was officially speechless for the first time that night. He knew how I felt about fraternizing in the office. He also knew that despite popular belief, I don't sleep around. As a matter of fact, it's been nearly a year since my last sexual encounter, well besides today of course.

"No shit, you are pulling my leg right?"

"Nope, it happened." I said to him as the images of Nicole and her chocolate drop nipples floated through my mind. I couldn't help but recall the way her skin tasted, sweet just like I knew it would. My dark skinned beauty. I've watched her from afar for the past few months. The way her hips sway when she walks, the way her smile lights up the room, even her work ethics were impressive. My desire for her was surprising for me. A man in my position didn't fuck his employees when he knew he had nothing to offer them. That was a lawsuit waiting to happen. I hoped like hell that Nicole wasn't one of those women looking to gain something by ruining my reputation. I'd done that all by myself as soon as my lips touched hers. I'd never been with a black woman before but now that I've had a taste of her sweetness, I don't know how I will be able to resist sampling more of her delectable sweet berries.

www.ingramcontent.com/pod-product-compliance
Lightning Source LLC
Chambersburg PA
CBHW071510170626
46811CB00007B/2803